10,000 Pink Birds of Love

Suzan G Brydon

ISBN: 978-0-9971984-1-6

Events in this book are purely fictional and not based on any
persons living or dead.

Even you, you butt-munch.

To my BDB and my fellow Pollyanna-realists:
love is real, love gets real.
Love yourself and one another.

Acknowledgements

There were many things I didn't know about writing books when I began this one. As soon as you tell people you're writing a book, the first thing they ask is what it's about. The second thing they ask you is if the characters are based on real people with whom you interact. The third thing they ask you, regardless of your answer to the second question, is to let them know when you're writing the next one so they can avoid you like the plague. Also, at all draft reviews your husband wants to understand which character represents him so he knows whether or not to be proud, pissed, or jealous. (Honey, I had to sprinkle bits and pieces of you into all of the characters, because your personality is just too gigantic for any one character to contain. That's my story, and I'm sticking to it.)

What I *did* know going in was that it would take the warm support of many friends and loved ones, as well as the kindness of strangers, in order for me to complete it (better, to get it to an acceptable point of done-ness, and done is good, right Lenore?). To my BDB, Schanno, Lisa K, my mama, and all the rest of you who so graciously served as early readers, editors, and, in some cases, inspiration for character development: thanks for your willingness to invest time in me, as well as your efforts to provide constructive criticism without falling back on, "Sorry, your baby is just ugly." And, thank you for reals to Hud-Bud for inspiring Oliver's quirks and for being a co-believer in the power of the Backfro. To Mike C. – you're a good man and a good friend. Beyond the on-call early reads and exceptional cover art you so unselfishly provided, you actually contributed something much greater: the encouragement and confidence boost I so desperately needed to dig deep, push hard, and believe I had something interesting to say. Warren Buffett once said, "It's better to hang out with people better than you. Pick out associates whose behavior is better than yours and you'll drift in that direction." Now you know why I want to hang out all the time.

For any ephemeral but impactful puffs of inventiveness you stumbled into in my writing, you can thank Radiohead. Thanks should also go to The Wolf Public House (now The Wolf Café) and the fantastic people there for allowing me the time, space, and hot coffee required to bring the story to its fruition…and, of course, for opening my eyes to such an ideal setting within which someone might successfully entertain others and/or be publicly humiliated.

Finally, for you whose actions and interactions inspired this book, you know who you are. Thank you for opening various doors to me at just those right moments when I needed to enter or exit. With trials and tribulations come compassion and growth, and through our exchanges, you have helped me gather plenty of it all. For a multitude of reasons, I am indebted to you. However, next time, perhaps work on being less of an ass.

Chapter 1

The steel girders were glacial, beaded with cold, semi-solid droplets. Each time a piece of Lloyd's exposed skin touched them he shuddered from the temperature and height. He tugged the straps again and squinted into the distance. It was time. His eyes filled with light and he smiled. He looked down, took a deep breath, spread his arms wide, hands clutching two giant trash bags, and prepared to let go.

It was at that precise moment a dual-wheeled Ford F150 filled with raucous teenagers, the type who play baseball with mailboxes, barreled across the bridge. Their passing created an updraft strong enough to disturb his footing. Startled, he turned, slipped, and dropped. His arms instinctively flailed toward the railing causing the garbage bags he was holding to fling high into the air above him. In a split second he found himself suspended mid-air, immobile, a dangling marionette. Surrounding him was a swirl of pink birds circling his head like leaves.

At first, all Lloyd could hear was the blood pumping in his eardrums. Then a car door slam, someone calling for the police, yelling, sirens in the distance, more car doors, more raised voices. Reluctantly, he opened an eye.

Shit.

So this is how it ends, he thought.

A crowd of gawkers, a freezing wind, a lost love, and, me dangling 30 feet above the parkway.

Of all nights to be wearing pink lycra.

Chapter 2

The dead don't make formal requests to be acknowledged by those they leave behind. A dead man's shadow-presence confronts whomever it wants, wherever it wants. It is limitless. It cannot be contained. It simply demands: *This was me. I was here. I am here still, and I will be heard.*

That was why Lloyd wanted to be dead.

The desire grew stronger as the water froze the surface of his eyes. Objects floated directly in front of him, but he could see nothing except a dull white glow. Recent memories flashed in and out of his consciousness, interrupted only by small chunks of ice brushing his face. Arguing with Beatrice about pickup rituals at daycare. Kissing his son on the forehead in his mother's kitchen before he raced out the door an hour ago. Agonizing over the precise order of the playlist he sketched out in his car: *Rachel Yamagata before or after Bruce Springsteen post-"The Ghost of Tom Joad?" Which would pluck her heartstrings in just the right rhythm for a sweet serenade to reverberate through her body? Should he send a playlist, burn a CD, or go really old school and somehow create a beloved mix tape?* He knew they both had strong affinities for mix tapes; that passion originated years ago when walking through middle school hallways playing mix tapes on a Walkman made both the mix tapes and their owners extraordinarily cool.

Lloyd wished he had known middle-school-Bea, and thinking of her then got him lost in a new train of thought. *Little Bea-Bea with the early 80s feathered bangs, streaked with green and blond from a combination of chlorine and Sun-In. Her nose peeling from summertime bike-riding, doing cartwheels across her parents' back patio, and spending hours mastering "Night Driver" on her Atari. What songs would have melted her heart back then? What about now? And, in the now, what precise moment is the right one to give the musical creation to her? Would she climb into my car with me to listen to it? Would my front seat feel inviting to her? Is my car clean? Did I lock the door when I got out? Did I double-check that I locked the door when I got out? Should I go double check it now? Could I phone in a sick day on Monday, if (or better, "when") this penultimate plan is successful? What will my boss say if I'm not at my desk by 9 a.m.? Knowing I said brightly as I left Friday - as I've said every Friday for three years - that I was spending the weekend reconciling with my wife, what will my boss say when I do show up at my desk by 9 a.m.?*

These questions swirled as tangibly around Lloyd as the icy liquid around his temples. The pain was excruciating, and the frigidity of the water made holding his breath incredibly difficult. He knew he'd have to let go soon, succumb.

It felt like hours passed, days. He was briefly convinced he had already been suspended in this arctic tomb for a millennia. Dead now, he thought. His key to being heard. It was time to capitulate. It was time to throw in the monogrammed bath towels. It was-

It was nearly thirty seconds before his best friend, Harold, realized Lloyd had dunked his head into the beer tub. Grabbing Lloyd by the collar Harold jerked him up. Icy droplets flung on nearby party-goers who raised their gazes disinterestedly from the artichoke dip to see who had splashed them from the pool. Lloyd let out a loud, wet gasp.

Harold stared blankly at him, still grasping him by the frozen shirt collar. He shook his head slightly then spoke slowly as he brought his beer toward his mouth. "Bro. Seriously. I'll assume this means you know the Capital B has arrived," he said taking a drink. "I'll also assume this was part of some brilliant plan you worked up earlier today and not some bizarre way to rid yourself of hyperthermia since it's like 90 fucking degrees today." Harold let go of Lloyd's collar and whacked him on the back of the head while Lloyd blinked slowly and worked to process the fact that he wasn't dead. He was just divorced.

Unlike the dead, Lloyd had realized recently – much to his chagrin – that divorced people were required to compare their perceptions against those of others, to submit to mediation, to seek consensus. The divorced must negotiate. They no longer had the luxury to assume their "others" would agree with or confirm them; that surface politeness dissolved when the marriage did. At every turn, they now found they needed to barter, to craft logical arguments just to work through the simplest of things, even if inside they were really only asking, "Is this okay with you as an individual person now that I can't deprive you of sex till I get what I want?" or, "Would you consider that, please, or do I need to hire another attorney?" They were obligated to debate reality even when things appeared obvious; obvious at least to one of the sides negotiating. So, so clear. As clear as the piercing blue of Beatrice's eyes, which, at this point, were making their way across the yard directly toward him. And, as always, those eyes were accompanied by the rest of her, as well as her best friend, Zoe.

"Well if it isn't the Queen B and her droning co-worker," Harold smirked at his own cleverness as he threw his empty bottle toward a nearby recycling bucket. It missed, and, fortunately, bounced into the grass instead of onto the concrete near the pool. He did his best to act nonchalant as he reached down to pick it up.

Zoe, walking slightly in front of Bea, used the long red nail on her middle finger to push Harold aside and reached into the cooler for a drink. "Better droning than cloning, ya reckon?" Zoe whipped her head back, the ends of her hair snapping Lloyd in the chin. "Like you two wankers," she said, looking both guys over and gesturing toward their shirts, "who apparently got a two-for-one special on shirts at Walmart or something."

Harold looked from his horizontal striped polo to Lloyd's and back, then stormed off mumbling obscenities in the air. Bea, on the other hand, ignored the entire exchange and stared at Lloyd who stood slack-jawed defrosting in the sunlight. Seeing Beatrice standing right in front of him he still remained somewhat convinced he was dead.

Bea leaned into Lloyd, shooting quick, peripheral glances around the pool. She whispered sternly to him through gritted teeth, "What-are-you-*doing*-here? You knew I was going to be here. You heard me telling Oliver when I dropped him off yesterday that I was coming to Gabby's house today. Why would you come here?" She tried on a fake smile for the nearby party goers. "And why on God's green earth are you so wet?"

Lloyd tried to chuckle. "Hey, there. Well, b-both easy questions," Lloyd stammered through pale blue lips. "B-because they're *our* friends and because, uh, it's pretty toasty today and I-I was working the crowd just before you got here. Life of the party; you know how I am." He lightly shook his head in hopes of clearing his thoughts, and it knocked off a tiny, stray ice cube stuck to his earlobe.

"Oh, really?" Bea said, suspiciously. "Since when have you treated Gabby and John like friends? Since the ten years *we've* received invitations to their party and *you've* never come with me?"

"How many times do I need to tell you?" Lloyd was defrosted enough now to press play on his social outing script. "I've changed, Bea. Besides, I know you love surprises."

"I love to be surprised by *people* I love with *things* I love. I don't love being surprised by someone I have *no* relationship with doing things I find *appalling*, Lloyd."

Lloyd tried his most penetrating and romantic stare, or at least the only one he could manage with icicles in his eyelashes. "We'll always have a relationship, Bea-Bea. Always." As her lip started to curl, he thought it best to throw in, "We have Oliver, remember?" with a light-hearted smile. "Now, go have fun with our friends."

Bea raised her eyebrows and snorted a laugh. "Yes, speaking of Oliver, we'll talk about that tomorrow. He misses you, Lloyd, so when it's your weekend you shouldn't be ditching him to come find-, to waste time in unusual places."

Lloyd shuddered slightly, hoping for contact as he saw her reach her arm forward, then he heard the clink of the bottle she was pulling out of the cooler and felt her withdraw from his space. He exhaled quietly.

"See you later!" he yelled brightly at her back as she walked away.

Zoe stared at him as she walked backwards, flicked her cigarette his direction, and saluted him before trotting to catch up with Bea.

Lloyd paused, exhaled, and shook droplets from his hair like a wet dog, his resolve renewed by his devout immersion in the cooler. Somehow he could make Beatrice hear him, truly hear him, without resorting to death. How could she not hear him when his feelings ran so deep? He would shout it from the rooftops…perhaps after thawing out a little. So he experienced a slight glitch in his plan. Not a problem. Monday morning, when he got to work, he would simply sync his phone to his Outlook calendar, Gantt chart, and whatever other tools he needed in order to identify the next best opportunity to reach Bea.

Harold returned to Lloyd's post by the cooler, licking dip off his paper plate and shaking his head. "Man, how many times do I need to tell you? You have *got* to let that bitch go. Grow a spine. Get over it. And while you're at it, can you not read a fucking calendar? What is today? It's the twentieth. Twen-ti-eth. An *even* day. *Even.* I told you not to wear that shirt on even days. You're odd days, *odd.* That deal was sealed at Target, my friend." They both looked toward Zoe and Bea as Harold found a final fingerful of dip to lick off his collar. "And what the hell does 'wanker' actually mean, anyway?"

Chapter 3

As the sun set an hour later Zoe sang loudly and traversed the edge of the driveway as if on a balance beam, arms stretched, making her way toward Bea's car. Fall in the Midwest brought kaleidoscopic views at sunset, but Bea was oblivious, watching her steps and silently fuming.

"'*Where'd you park your car? Where'd you park your car?... Walking, walking, walking.*'" Zoe sang to the sky. "I mean, who plays Radiohead at an afternoon pool party, really. Bloody brilliant! May we ask them to host our next department party?"

Once in the car, Bea scanned over her shoulder and backed her car out onto Portulaca Drive. She interrupted Zoe's out-of-tune, albeit heartfelt, singing. "I cannot believe he showed up. I mean, when is he going to get it through his head that we're over, you know?"

"'*I wanted to tell you but you never listened. I wanted to tell you but you never listened.*'" Zoe bounced her head around singing to herself. "Oh, as if!" she yelled.

Bea stopped the car and stared at Zoe incredulously. "What do you mean?"

"Of course you can believe he showed up! In fact, lovey, I think you secretly want him to show up everywhere you go, you little drama queen."

"I beg your pardon?" Bea looked nauseous as she put the car in drive. "Okay. I think I just vomit-burped in my mouth a little."

Zoe laughed. "Aww, I'm just taking the piss out of ya, sweet pea. No one could seriously want that git to show up anywhere except to his own funeral." Zoe pouted her lips at the visor as she freshened up her lipstick.

Bea chuckled and loosened her shoulders. "Possibly true, but a little harsh, don't you think? Remember, I have Oliver to think about. Granted, fantasizing about his funeral might keep me from hurling, but sadly, it's probably not be the best thing that could happen for Oliver."

"Yeah, yeah. Ollie'd be fine. He's young; he'd get over the loss soon enough," Zoe patted Bea's leg and they both smiled. "But seriously though, you are way too nice about it. You didn't even really give him a hard time about being there!"

Bea turned her attention from the road long enough to glare at Zoe. "I did, too! You were there! You watched me!"

"Yeah, I watched you kind of stand there all close to him, flitting your eyes about and everything."

Bea shot her best pissed-off look. "I didn't flit! There was no flitting! I rolled my eyes at him when he gave me his lame excuse about having the same friends and how he's changed and—"

"—Look, don't get your knickers in a knot. All I'm saying," Zoe interrupted, "is that maybe you're too soft to him. It sends the wrong message, you know? If the message you want to send is 'It's over,' he ain't getting it, sweetheart. You need to be a bit more forceful. Give it heaps." Bea stared straight ahead at the road, frowning. "Next time you see him, just glare at him and poke your finger in his chest, like this,"

Zoe used her middle finger to thump just below Bea's throat repeatedly, "and say, 'Look, wanker, it's over, okay? I know you've had perfection and it's hard to cope without it, but get over it, you know? Get on with your life. Grow up, and get on with your business.' And, if that doesn't work, try kicking him in the balls. Works with dogs."

Bea snickered as Zoe pulled up "Morning Bell" on her iPod and sang along from the beginning, but, she knew she was now destined for a dour night out. First, she'd be terrified that wherever they went, they'd run into Lloyd again, since Oliver was no doubt with Lloyd's mother. Again. That created an automatic level of discomfort. Second, whether or not she agreed with anything Zoe said, she'd carry some of the "flitting" guilt with her throughout the night. Zoe suggested it and now it was out there, imagined or not. Even if there was no flitting. And there was no flitting. Absolutely none. Third, she was angry that Lloyd had obviously asked his mother to watch Oliver while he went out in search of her, yet again. And she knew Oliver would be upset when she picked him up tomorrow. Oliver loved his grandmother and Bea knew he was in good hands. But, she also knew Oliver felt he wasn't getting enough one-on-one time with his dad over the last few months. Fourth, and finally, she had "vurped" cheap, watery beer into her mouth before she and Zoe went to flit, or flirt with men she might *actually* be interested in, and she was quite particular about oral hygiene. All four presented a strong list of reasons to simply turn the car around, drop Zoe off, and go home to watch Sandra Bullock movies and flip through dating websites. But promises had been made, legs had been shaved, and *Radiohead* à la Zoe was in rare form, so the car maintained its trajectory toward pubs and late-night philosophical laments on love. Or perhaps just hours of beer pong.

Bea and Zoe pulled up at The Ballroom at that unique Saturday-evening time when middle-agers are enjoying a few precious hours of babysitting and twenty-somethings have yet to shower and go out for the night. Having just been allowed to grab food and a few minutes of baseball fanaticism at the Fox and Hound, Bea felt obliged to humor Zoe by bringing her here. Zoe didn't hide her disdain for televised sports or the men who become absorbed in them, but, her love for Bea always took precedence, so she spent her time attempting to distract Bea with Buzztime trivia while Bea polished off toasted ravioli and cheered her Cardinals to a victory. Once the game was over, however, Zoe wasted no time pulling Bea out of the sports den and on to bigger and better things.

Walking into The Ballroom Bea headed directly for the bar, or as it was called there, the "Retoxication Station," and snagged two cold ones while Zoe surveyed the surroundings. As always, Zoe smiled at passing patrons in an attempt to identify possible drink benefactors. Bea was continually amazed at what little money Zoe spent on drinks. It was as if Zoe was a living, breathing pub game to which most – men and women alike - became easily addicted and put their money into with fervor. Chat a bit and you're hooked. Try her once and you found yourself unable to stop putting drinks in her simply because of a desire to keep her around longer. Bea considered it a true gift and counted herself among the addicted.

The Ballroom was aptly named for its massive collection of pool tables adjacent the bar, pinball machines lining the walls, and beer pong tables near the front windows. And, although Bea and Zoe were by no means league-worthy players in any of those areas, they opted to insert quarters into one of the open pool tables. Why? Because they were keenly aware that at that particular moment they both inhabited "the Zone," which as any good pool-playing bar hopper knows, is that time during a night out when you've had just enough drink to relax your breaks and bank shots but not so much that you hit the cloth instead of the cue ball. Therefore, Bea and Zoe began to play, the pub began its crawl toward capacity, and soon all tables were taken.

The Zone ran wide and deep for a few hours. Bea managed to mysteriously create backwards English on her cue ball at least once, and Zoe sank four solids in a row. In the middle of high-fiving as the fifth ball sank, two Farmhouse fraternity brothers wearing Cargill seed hats approached them and asked if they could take the table. When Bea and Zoe initially declined, they upped the ante, offering to pay for the next game if they could play, winner taking the table going forward.

"Right on, boys," Zoe said. "But, let's make it the game plus a pint for the winners." She smiled coyly and winked at Bea while she chalked her cue, "unless of course you're a tiny bit frightened."

Bea shook her head at them abashedly, hoping to keep the night within her budget.

"Bring it, your majesty," the one in the Cargill cap said with a bow.

"Great. We get to pay you to make us look bad," Bea said mostly to herself and shrugged, as Cargill-cap-guy lined up his first shot.

The frat boys began their game in earnest, but lost quickly in embarrassment. After bringing over two fresh beers to beaming Bea and Zoe, two new contenders approached. Same offer, same result. Soon, the table began to draw observers. Zoe began to hold court, tossing her winnings toward young male patrons sitting nearby and asking them to play The Verve on the jukebox, this of course was something she would never do prior to downing three pints as she swore, when sober, that the reviewer's descriptions of them as "spellbinding" were "trite and exaggerated." Tonight, however, Zoe danced and sang devotedly into her cue stick, yet still managed to make every shot.

"Three in a row, my friends! Lucky number three!" Zoe shouted loudly into the bar. "I hereby pronounce that whoever shall challenge us next so doeth at great peril, for they shall be required to open thine tab to us."

Bea smiled and held up a timeout signal to Zoe. She made her way through the packed pub toward the restroom, leaving three full drinks and Zoe ordering her next playlist by yelling at anyone who went near the jukebox. Emerging from the ladies room relieved and chuckling, Bea was weaving her way back toward the pool table when a segment of conversation from a small group by the bar wafted her way.

"Yeah, I'm gonna pay for my drink then see what's up. Apparently there's two chicks over there hustling for pool and messing around with other chicks' boyfriends. I heard someone's about to go bust their asses."

Bea's eyes widened in shock. "No! No! That's not what-" she tried to yell over the din, but knew it was pointless. Instead she pushed against the crowd, zig-zagging methodically back to the table. Once there, she glanced quickly around, then whispered as nonchalantly as possible to Zoe that this was, undoubtedly, the best time to leave.

"Well, it has been a real pleasure, gentlemen, a real pleasure. It appears, however, we have to be somewhere else. Another time, perhaps." Zoe said as she bowed deeply, put her cue stick in the hand of a random observer, her check and some cash into the hand of a waiter passing by, and allowed herself to be pulled by the forearm toward the door.

Quiet, grumbled complaints about where the two floozy pool sharks went, how much money was actually lost, and who now owned the table grew into louder discontent, but Bea and Zoe were too busy crouching low and weaving in and out of the crowd as they worked their way toward the door to notice the changing vibe. Although Zoe's rendition of The Verve's *Bittersweet Symphony* escalated into its second verse and indicated she was oblivious to the gravity of the changing tide, Bea remained a woman on a mission.

"Stay low, make no eye contact, and get the hell out of here," she repeatedly whispered. Bea kept them skirting around stools and ducking under arms as quickly as she could. She picked up their pace when she finally spotted the exit. When at last they reached the front door, Bea pressed her shoulder into it, head down, and burst with force into the outside world pulling Zoe directly behind.

Unfortunately, unbeknownst to Bea, the other side of the front door was occupied, and Bea and Zoe toppled directly onto the man walking in. All three of them fell like dominos onto the soaked pavement: the newcomer flat on his back, Bea face-flat against his torso still grasping Zoe's arm, and Zoe teetered on Bea like a turtle on its shell.

"Oh God, I'm so sorry," Bea's voice was muffled as her

face was pressed into the man's stomach. Zoe continued singing her coda from atop Bea's back.

"No, no. It's totally my fault. I, uh, I guess I should have opened the door first and announced loudly that I was entering," the man gasped, as he regained his breath and spit strands of Bea's long blond hair out of his mouth.

"It's just, there was this big misunderstanding in there and we were trying to get out as quickly as possible because…well, it's a long story," Bea tried clumsily to recover her balance and pull back onto her knees. She turned her head enough to say "Zoe, get off!", but Zoe had just shifted her *Bittersweet Symphony* into a falsetto and seemed oblivious to their horizontal state.

"Bea? Bea Stanley?"

It wasn't until he said her name that Bea actually looked up at their victim. Her eyes opened wide and her face softened into a smile. "Sam?"

"Yeah! Hey! Gosh, I haven't seen you in, what, like six or seven years, right?"

"At least! How are you?"

"I'm good, I'm good. Still racing, still working hard. You?"

Suddenly Bea remembered her single state and how attractive Sam actually was, and she flushed with embarrassment. She pushed backward with all her might and sat on her heels, brushing Guinness-soaked gravel off her hands onto her pant legs whilst sending Zoe sliding backwards onto the pavement. Bea ignored her and casually fluffed her hair. "I'm great. Really good, actually. I'm still working at the university. Wait, was I working there when we last talked?"

Finally, Zoe's singing paused. "Hey, kids. Are we gonna

camp out here all night and cuddle or are we actually going to get up at some point and grab another pint?"

"Oh, God, yeah, sorry. Here, let me help you," Bea said to Sam as she stood up, reaching her hand toward him and knocking Zoe onto her bottom with a thud.

"No, I got it," Sam said standing up and holding Bea's hand, though he clearly had his balance. Their hands stayed clasped slightly longer than necessary.

"Oh, bloody hell," Zoe mumbled as she finally winched her own way up and hobbled off to the car. "I'll be waiting to go get that drink when you're ready, lovey."

"Yeah, okay," Bea yelled over her shoulder without taking her eyes off Sam. Questions quickly began and soon the two were deep into a game of catch-up about local businesses, shared friends, and changes that only decades-old acquaintances in a small city can have. When it felt they had run out of basic niceties to discuss, Bea paused and smiled. "Well. So. I guess I should be going. Sorry again for the, you know, unannounced exit."

"Yeah. Sure, no problem. I, uh," Sam looked sheepishly at the ground. "I can't help but notice that you're not wearing a wedding ring. Did you wager it in there during a game of pool?"

"Ha! Um, yeah, no," Bea laughed. "I'm, uh, I'm divorced now," Bea said with a half-smile.

"Oh. Sorry to hear that."

"Yeah, well, it's not unusual, right? It happens all the time," she glanced around. "But, it was definitely for the best, I think. We're both better off," she said with an awkward smile.

"That's good, I guess. So…does that mean you might be

open to dinner sometime?"

Bea looked at him tentatively. The flush in her cheeks reminded her how much she liked interacting with Sam years ago when he came to the bookstore. She had always found him attractive and tried on numerous occasions to introduce him to single women she knew at the time. Now she was the single woman.

"Um, okay. Sure. Yeah. Why not?" she smiled. They exchanged numbers, and just as Bea was putting his into her phone a text popped up from Lloyd:

"Hey! :-) @ O'Riley's if u want 2 join us."

Startled, Bea quickly closed her phone, said goodbye to Sam, and headed for her car.

When she climbed in Zoe was grinning broadly. "Uh-huh. I saw you taking digits, sweet pea! Free beer, free pool, fantastic view of the stars, and a phone number for a shag fest. I'd call that a brilliant night, whaddya reckon'?"

Bea rolled her eyes in mock disdain and smiled at Zoe.

"Oh, and now you're flitting your eyes at *me*, you cheeky girl. You're insatiable! You just want everyone!"

At Zoe's reminder of her interaction with Lloyd and the subsequent text she received, the warmth in Bea's stomach she had previously attributed to excitement over the exchange with Sam turned into mild dread.

Chapter 4

Lloyd sat on his bar stool playing finger drums on his Budweiser bottle. His eyes were firmly fixed on the door, only darting away occasionally to check his phone for return texts from Bea. Harold belched loudly as he walked through the bar, pointing and winking at the bartender for punctuation. Upon returning from the restroom he smacked Lloyd hard enough on the back to make him choke on a peanut.

"Dude, let's get the fuck out of here. This place is hella-lame. *You* know she's not coming. *I* know she's not coming," he took a swig of beer. "At least she's not coming with you. Heh heh heh."

"Hi*lari*ous," Lloyd said, his eyes still glued to the entrance. "You don't know anything. And why do you care, anyway? What other plans could you possibly have? A Saturday night root canal? Head home to study the phasing problem on your high school marching band videos? Why are you in such a hurry?"

"I *do* know she's not coming. And, as I told you, my band was ahead of its time. Don't be a hater, bro."

"She's met me out before."

"Yeah. Twice in the past three years. Once when she was butt-wasted and yours was the only number she could remember, and once when she agreed to have a 'cordial'

dinner as friends 'for Oliver's sake.' You go, Casanova."
Harold clinked his bottle into Lloyd's.

Lloyd shot Harold a nasty look out of the corner of his
eye. "Really? Casanova? Is that the best you've got? Isn't there
anyone more nineteenth-century you could try and slam me
with?"

"Shut up. I made my point."

"If only I could hang out with Casanova" Lloyd mumbled
to himself. "Spend some valuable time with somebody who
could teach me a thing or two about women," he said as he
rubbed the label on his bottle. He looked toward the ceiling
wistfully. "You know, like a romance role model or
something. Some guy who could walk me through the steps
on how not to screw up with women. A modern day Eros. A
love guru. A director of destiny. Hell, I need a real life *Hitch*.
Where's Will Smith when a man really needs him, huh? A
teacher of how to woo Bea. That's what I need."

"Did I just hear you say 'woo', for real?" Harold snorted
and shook his head. "Now who's nineteenth century, my
friend?" He took a drink and slammed his bottle down. "Look,
all you need to be taught is how to ignore her. Be all cold and
distant and unavailable and shit. In fact, it's actually my life's
ambition to teach you how to be meaner to Bea. That way,
she'll either come running after you like some lost, sappy little
puppy, or you'll grow a pair and decide you don't need her.
The latter of course is my hope. Either way, train you I can,
my young Padawan. That way I get to channel my inner Yoda
while also having the good fortune of hanging out with some
dude who's not acting like a crying little bitch all the time." He
took another drink then smiled and raised his eyebrows at the
trio of thirty-something women down the bar who, by all

appearances, were celebrating a bachelorette night version 2.0. Upon receiving no response, Harold tried to act indifferent. He cleared his throat and shifted his focus to ESPN's Cardinals/Diamondbacks recap.

Lloyd reverted to watching the door. There was no sign of Bea busting through O'Riley's entrance, nor was there any movement through the flashing door that was his AT&T smartphone. *What the hell good would a "meanness mentor" do?,* he thought. *Dumbass. What I need is romance expertise. Like the classic angel-devil shoulder duo who whisper kernels of wooing wisdom and suggestions for tactical risks in my ear each time I ran into Bea. Like a personal, private theme-song band well-versed in the ins and outs of relationship management who could accompany me everywhere I went, bust in just before I entered a room where Bea was, and set the mood properly.* His Budweiser-bottle thumb-beats increased in intensity as he wracked his brain for an easy way to win her back.

One advantage of working for an old, family-owned business was that little attention was paid to how much bandwidth their employees used on personal interests. A plethora of Pandora and social networking sites sucked up gigabytes daily, and, if that breadth of entertainment wasn't enough to keep some folks at or around their desks, regular time spent in the cafeteria on Monday mornings playing "Match the Awkward Weekend Story to the Correct Cubicle Gopher" certainly took up a lot of time.

For a Monday Lloyd was abnormally disinterested in both of those time killers, but he was in no way jumping with joy into the financial transaction query requests piling up in his inbox. Instead he spent his first two hours sifting through Facebook for posts about Bea's weekend. Fortunately, after their separation Bea never "unfriended" him, and he frequently perused her posts to see what the hot buttons in her life were. On this particular Monday, he saw numerous post-weekend interactions on her page between Bea and her students filled with sentiments such as, "Hey! Sorry I missed class this morning. I was hung over. :-p" and he smiled. He remembered vividly what she looked like as she stood in their old master bath Monday nights for years complaining about those overly-revealing posts from her students. She loved that her students felt comfortable enough with her to share details from their personal lives. She hated that they had no filter and often told her things to which she wished she was oblivious, things she didn't know whether to call them out on or report. Lloyd recalled half-listening to her emotional turmoil when they were married and regretted not paying better attention.

Hoping to attain some interaction now, he took a deep breath and decided to send her a message with a link to a headline he knew she'd love from *The Onion*. "Commas, Turning Up, Everywhere." He decided to read it in full after sending it, and just before he reached the end of the final paragraph he was startled by his ringing phone. Looking down he saw the snapshot he had taken of Bea during a beach vacation in 2003, the picture that accompanied any incoming call from her, and his heart skipped a beat. He snatched the phone.

"Well, hello there!" he answered with a smile wide enough to be heard over the phone. "Wow! You read fast! Wasn't that hilarious?"

"Is that how you answer the phone all the time?" she

asked curtly. "I have absolutely no idea what you're talking about."

"Oh, sorry," Lloyd stumbled. "I- uh, I thought you were calling because of the link I just sent you." Silence. "It doesn't matter. I'm sure you'll get it late-"

"Link? What link?" Bea interrupted. "I haven't checked my email in hours. I'm slammed with grading today. Listen, I'm just multitasking and taking two seconds to plow through my home to-do list. It's about Oliver's invoice from the dentist. I would appreciate it if you could get me your fifty percent of the bill as soon as possible. I'm scraping up every possible cent to try and afford a special campsite at Bonnaroo by the time tickets go on sale in January."

"Cool! I should come with you and help you cut costs. I think I heard Beck was playing, right? Sounds fun!"

"You?" she said with a small chuckle. "Since when are *you* interested in Bonnaroo? Did you suddenly forget it has all the things you hate? Heat. Tents. 100,000 people. Music til 4am."

"Aw, c'mon. I love music, and I-, well I've been looking for a reason to use that battery-operated fan Mom re-gifted me last Christmas. I am so ready for Bonnaroo. Bonnaroo!" Lloyd said sincerely, although he knew she would interpret it differently. The only sound he heard on the other end was the shuffling of paper. Best to change the subject, he thought. "So, do anything fun this weekend?"

"Um," she sighed, "not a lot. Went to see the new Simon Pegg movie."

"Oh yeah? How was that?" he asked, smiling again as he recalled she had adored Simon Pegg ever since *Shaun of the Dead* was released. Bea firmly believed Rom-Zom-Coms were a highly under-appreciated genre.

"It was okay. The movie was kinda lacking in character development, but you know Simon Pegg always makes me laugh." Lloyd loved how Bea laughed anytime she said 'makes me laugh,' and her laugh touched his heart through the phone. It made him smile back. He had seen her students do it, too, in her office hours. It was impossible not to. If everything stopped here, he knew today would be a good day for them. He just needed to forego the opportunity to probe, and it could end on a high note.

"Was this a movie *and* a date?" he probed further. He couldn't resist. It was like a tic.

"Yep." Her voice reverted to being curt and the audible smile vaporized.

"Ah-ha. So you *are* dating again! Well, you know, if you're interested in dating, I know someone who is avail-" "Listen, Lloyd, I've got students coming to my office hours any minute, so if you could get your share of that invoice to me that would be great, and don't forget to check Oliver's homework folder when you pick him up Wednesday from school, okay? Thanks. Talk to you later." After no pause for a response, Bea quickly hung up.

Lloyd rested his head on his fingertips and stared at his cubicle wall. His eyes drifted across the weave. He stared so intently and for so long that the dark gray lines separating each miniature, light gray panel jumped towards him as if he were front row at an intense 3-D movie. An addictive optical illusion. He continued staring, pivoting slightly in his chair so the pixels seemed to dance forwards and backwards. Lloyd always felt frustrated when Bea stopped him from making his dating case to her. They still got along well, so he rationalized that if she was interested in dating -- and *he* was definitely interested -- for Oliver's sake they should try to go on a few dates again to see if they could regain some of their old momentum. He shook his head, baffled by her seeming inability to follow the inherent logic.

"Dude!"

Lloyd's arms grappled forward knocking his mouse off the sliding keyboard tray, and he sighed audibly as he crawled under his desk to pick it up.

"Harold, why do you insist on yelling every time you come over here?" Lloyd inquired from under his desk. "You know that scares the bejeezus out of me."

"Whatever, man, I never knew you were channeling Jesus, but right on. Maybe if you weren't doing shit you were afraid to get caught doing then you wouldn't be so uptight about everything all the time," Harold smirked.

"I wasn't doing anything," Lloyd said defensively as he reached his hand up from underneath the desk and quickly attempted to close Facebook.

Harold glanced at the screen. "Dude, are you cyber-stalking her again? Lame. For real. If you're gonna cyber-stalk someone why in the hell would you choose your ex-wife? I mean, c'mon on! There's Wendy down the hall. Even *she* knows she has a nice ass, and she's always posting pictures of herself laying out by her pool. Or maybe Cheree, who posts videos of her and her old sorority sisters dancing half-naked like every fifth day. But you...no, you decide to use the invisible cloak of the internet to be a fly on the wall at your ex-wife's house. Awesome."

"I'm not cyber-stalking anyone. I was just... reading. You know, just seeing what our friends are up to and what not."

"Yeah, reading. And, what not. Well, read this," Harold held a backwards "L" to his forehead. "And, it's not code for Lloyd, in case you're wondering."

"Are you finished?"

"Not even close, but seriously, if you wanna know stuff like intimate details why are you wasting your time surfing lame posts frat boys are making on her Facebook? You have a world of info at your fingertips to use as you see fit, Bro." Harold grinned, obviously pleased with his perceived genius.

"What are you getting at?"

"Don't you sit on your ass and look at data all fucking day, genius?"

"Yeah, what's your point?"

"And what kind of data, pray tell, do you look at all day?"

"Harold, you and I both do the same thing, for God's sake. Boring-as-fuck financial transaction analysis. Get to your point, if you have one, so I can actually get back to doing it." Lloyd pinched the bridge of his nose and closed his eyes.

"Well, Maestro, instead of watching Dave Jones's VISA account all damn day to see how much gold he buys on World of Warcraft just so we can write a report that tells IGE how to increase their revenue stream, why don't you see what *she* is up to?"

Lloyd glared at Harold incredulously. "What?! No way! I'm not going to tap into her debit card account and play Big Brother, you idiot."

"Why the hell not? You do it to everyone else."

"I do it to everyone else because my job requires I do data analysis for our clients, remember? What it *doesn't* require is independently monitoring my ex-wife's spending patterns."

Harold threw his hands up and backed away. "Alright,

whatever man, but don't come bitching to me when you're obsessed with what she's doing next weekend when you know all it takes is two keystrokes to find out she's going to a B&B in wine country with some history professor douchebag. All I'm saying is, remember that teenage chick in the news whose family found out she was pregnant because Target sent ads for diapers and cribs and shit to her house? All because she was buying, like, lingerie and lube and a pregnancy test? Predictive analysis, my friend. The wave of the stalker's future," Harold wiggled his eyebrows up and down. He turned to walk down the hall and shouted over his shoulder, "I'll see you at Oishi's. Sashimi. 1pm. You're buying."

"Yeah, sure," Lloyd said as he finally opened his inbox to do actual work.

Creating the custom SQL for his initial query required him to pull in the "date of purchase" and "merchant location" fields from one of their client's data, and his eyes meandered again over the gray fabric field fencing him in as he considered the repercussions of these new investigative possibilities Harold had now cemented in his mind.

Chapter 5

She had no idea how he managed it, but five minutes of talking with Lloyd doubled Bea's stomach acid production. Her fight-or-flight response always kicked into high gear, and the next thing she knew she found herself bunkered in the fifth floor women's restroom courtesy-flushing every five minutes. As she hung up on Lloyd this time Bea had automatically reached into her drawer for Tropical Fruit Tums, chewing two strawberry-flavored ones quickly and trying to pick them out of her teeth before her noon meeting. It didn't matter whether the conversation was filled with relaxed laughs or vociferous complaining, the outcome was always the same. Her heart rate increased, the lining of her stomach burned, and she'd forget to breathe normally. That's why, as bad as she felt about being short when talking with him on occasion, she cut herself slack knowing the damage inflicted on her delicate nervous system outweighed the slight irritation he might experience due to her curt demeanor.

Today she realized *she* created the problem by calling him from her office, her sanctuary. She took a deep breath, closed her eyes, and tried to regroup. The only sounds were the low rumble of hallway exchanges outside her office and water trickling through the Zen meditation fountain perched on the third shelf of her bookcase. Her office was peaceful, serene. She breathed deeply again and smelled the fresh flowers and vanilla she consistently kept nearby both at work and home Sitting quietly, just breathing in the midst of all her books, listening to the water, anticipating the new things she learned through every student interaction. All of this helped her find her center again. Unlike some of her female colleagues who swore work stressed them beyond belief and wanted nothing more than to stay home full-time, Bea loved work. She even hesitated to use the word "work" and tended toward loftier descriptions like "vocation," "calling," or sometimes even "escape."

She loved teaching, loved her students, loved to write and research. Her workspace, albeit mentally and physically challenging in its own way, was devoid of electric bills, toilets that needed to be cleaned, and clingy, amorous partners who begged for her to complete them. Work-Bea was her favorite persona. Work-Bea spoke with candor and confidence in the classroom and on committees. Work-Bea built respect with her peers through her writing. Work-Bea brought multi-faceted Bea the majority of her peace and contentment, even when wading daily through piles of student papers and excuses. In fact, Work-Bea hid the fact that she usually found the papers moving and the excuses humorous; a secret she kept from most students and colleagues.

Despite frequently toiling over papers until 2 a.m. to offer thorough feedback, or searching piles of articles and textbooks to find the best example to motivate a straggler to push the boundaries, the effort felt warm, predestined, comfortable. It suggested home. Bea even felt fraudulent at times, wondering how it was that someone, somewhere had decided to pay her for doing something she loved so much; and in those middle-of-the-night, angst-ridden moments, the fear that raised its ugly head most frequently was that someone would call "shenanigans." That somehow an administrator would drop by her office to say "Yes, Dr. Stanley, we're glad you had a good time, but that's quite enough. Time to stop playing school now and get on to a real job."

Bea opened her eyes again, took a deep breath, and made the mental leap back into her pile of grading. Her earlier distress about the phone call soon subsided, and the day returned to feeling particularly homey. Around 9:00 am, students appeared one-by-one every half hour to review drafts of their capstone essays. Spending hours exploring personal stories to help people communicate more effectively was as good as it gets as far as Bea was concerned. As a first generation college student teaching at the least expensive university in the state, she quite often encountered those that reminded her of her younger self. She could relate to the students even though their ability to remind her of her own flaws often meant old wounds stayed unhealed, regularly bandaged, and occasionally itchy. She knew the demons that haunted them. Feelings of uncertainty and insecurity haunted them, having kicked and clawed their ways Podunk Nowhere to the halls of higher education. They lacked the confidence of those whose families sent generations of offspring to rigorous boarding schools, something she and her students liked to poke fun at, yet secretly envied.

As she waited for the last student to arrive for his appointment, Bea stopped to check her email. In between a call for papers at the next regional conference and a Buzztime Trivia Eblast from The Replay Bar and Grill was a new personal email, and not just any new email. This one was from Sam. When she saw his name on her screen a wave of heat hit her cheeks and her mouth crinkled around the edges uncontrollably.

"That must be some message." Zoe had poked her head in the doorway.

"I have no idea. I haven't read it yet." She smiled broadly. "Is it that obvious?"

"Mmm, now we see what makes the doctor blush, eh? A little textual intercourse," Zoe teased.

"It's only an email," Bea shrugged.

"Well, at least open it and spill it before I let Sparky in for his 12:30 appointment. That way I won't have to hound you later for all the juicy details."

Bea opened the message. It was an invitation to a "make-up dinner." She and Sam had already tried a first date after their unexpected bar encounter, and the results had been, well, less than stellar. They went to an Italian restaurant and she ignored everything he did and said for the first hour. To be fair, she assumed he could find a way not to take that personally because, to be fair, it was playoff season and the game was broadcasting on every screen in the joint. She was a little slow to pick up on his embarrassment as she leapt up from the table and yelled loudly in the middle of the restaurant when her beloved St Louis Cardinals won the game. That mediocre dinner was followed by a trip to a local pub where some woman kept sending Sam drinks accompanied by bar-napkin messages via the waitress. He was so intent on wracking his brain to determine when he had met this mystery woman he hadn't been fully aware of Bea's disengagement. Suffice it to say, neither left feeling great about the evening, and together they chalked it up to something in the air that night.

"He offered to cook me dinner at his place," she told Zoe.

"Oooooh! Cheeky monkey wants to get you alone and closer to his bedroom, apparently," Zoe winked and made smoochy sounds. "That's one way to get things back on track."

Bea rolled her eyes but smiled broadly, her cheeks flushed as she tried to yell "Michael, you're up!" into the hallway in an attempt to trump Zoe's voice as she began an off-key rendition of "It's Getting Hot in Herre."

Chapter 6

There are valuable, legitimate reasons grown men don't typically wear masks when entering Wal-Mart. First, it's much harder to take in all the choices an aisle offers up if you don't have full use of your peripherals. Second, in a city the size of Chesterfield, you frequently run into old high school friends and, really, how could you expect them to believe you are reasonably successful – and straight - if you are wearing black vinyl and pointy ears? Third, while potentially cool and infinitely mysterious, it is understood that sometimes people don't have the best intentions when they work to hide their true identities. Take Lex Luthor, for example. Or Count Duku. Mystery shoppers, perhaps. The Trix rabbit.

Lloyd's eyebrows raised hopefully as he articulated some version of this last point to Oliver through his Malibu's rear view mirror. He continued this logical, heartfelt explanation as he parked his car in the spot beside the cart return, but he could still sense the disappointment on Oliver's face, despite the fact that nearly all of that face was concealed by a mask. As always, his son's sadness caused significant upset in Lloyd. Sighing, he pivoted in his seat.

"Okay. I'll make you a deal. How about you wear the mask and cape and I carry the wand?"

Oliver tilted his head skeptically, "Yeah, but what are you going to *do* with the wand?"

Lloyd wavered. "I'm uh, well…I'm gonna use the force to ward off Darksiders, of course!" he said with enthusiasm.

"Dad, that's Star Wars! That's not Harry Potter!" Oliver complained. "Mom practices her spells at the store. You know, like 'Alohomora!' and 'Expecto Patronum!' and 'Enervate', or something like that when people walk by. But not the evil ones," he cautioned. Lloyd smiled at the way Oliver bragged about his mom but also felt a little sick to his stomach.

"Yeah, Mommy's good like that," Lloyd agreed, wistfully.

For Oliver's fourth birthday, he had begged for a Harry-Potter-themed party. Bea had stayed up until well after two a.m. on that Friday working to shape Oliver's birthday cake into a Gryffindor coat of arms, complete with elaborate wrinkles around the lion's mouth. A few hours later, she jumped up to speed-clean the house and herself before party guests arrived. Lloyd remembered watching her stand in her graduation robe in their master bathroom for what seemed like forever painstakingly putting Hermione-like ringlets into each strand of her long hair and practicing spells before families arrived. Bea sought to please, and her determination, creativity, and sometimes unhealthy perfectionism were something to behold. He adored her then, her jeans and Chucks visible below the hem of her black robe as she silently recited those made-up spells. He adored her no less now, just blocks away from where they had left her when he picked Oliver up for the weekend.

"Dad!"

"What? Sorry. Daydreaming. Are you ready to go in?"

"Yeah, but are you going to do the *spells?*" Oliver whined.

"Yep, just like Mommy."

"*And* ride on the cart?"

"Yep, just like Mommy."

"Deal!" Oliver yelled as he unbuckled his shrinking car seat.

"Wouldn't it be cool if Mommy was here to play Sorcerer's Stone with us?" Lloyd said brightly over his shoulder, but his words reverberated against a slammed door, and he jumped out of the car terrified Oliver would fly his invisible broomstick in front of a Buick.

As they walked into Walmart Lloyd's eye inadvertently ticked as the tail of Oliver's cape narrowly escaped the automated door. Then he relaxed as he saw it fall in behind his son in the front of a truck-shaped grocery cart. Opening his wallet, he verbally scanned his grocery list.

"Okay, Buddy. Let's see. Since we're at Wal-Mart today we'll start in aisle eight, which as we both know, is where they keep the awesome peanut butter with no peanuts and extra gooey jelly for tomorrow's lunch. Then, we go to aisles nine and ten for Frosted Flakes, coffee for Daddy, Juicy Juice for Oliver, and spaghetti with white cheese. We skip aisle eleven this week cause we don't need any more candy or treats, and we go directly to aisles twelve through fourteen for milk, lunchmeat, frozen veggies, toasted ravioli, and of course, your all-time favorite: chicken nuggets. Then, we circle back around for aisles one through seven for fruit and fresh veggies and we're out the door. Sound good? Pretty cool that I have a spreadsheet that tells me what's in each aisle, huh?" Lloyd said with gusto.

"Yeah, I'm not a baby, Dad. You don't have to say Juicy Juice. It's just juice." Oliver continued rambling distractedly. "Last week, Mommy made us shu-shi. Shu-shi. Shu-shi! That sounds like a spell, doesn't it, Dad?" Oliver used his pointer finger to shoot spells at the canned goods.

"Really? No love for Dad on the list? Aww, come on. You have to admit it's pretty awesome I can predict where everything is, like magic! I'll bet you didn't think I knew where everything was."

"Yeah, I guess," Oliver agreed less-than-halfheartedly, searching the inside of the cart, "or we could just get black and white things."

"Black and white things?"

"Yeah. Or underwater things. When me and Mommy come to the store sometimes we have movie night and we have black and white night and we walk through the store and only put things in our basket that are black or white to eat, then we watch *101 Dalmatians.* Or underwater dinner night where we only look for things that look like coral and we shape our food to look like sharks and stuff and then we watch *Nemo.*" Oliver pronounced proudly before buckling himself into the driver's seat. "Mommy can tell you how it works, Dad."

"Yeah, well, not everyone can be Mommy, can they?" Lloyd sighed and pressed on to aisle eight. "Okay. Now which brand of peanut butter is it we like most? Do you remember? Maybe my wand can help me find it."

Lloyd hoped focusing on the wand would draw Oliver's attention away from what he knew to be a pained expression summoned by the mention of movie nights. It was Bea's idea about six years ago. They had just released the Pixar 3-pack-- *Toy Story*, *Toy Story 2*, and *A Bug's Life*--on DVD. Oliver was quite small and was just eating finger foods. Bea was so excited. It was a cold Saturday, and she thought it would be fun for them to spread a blanket in front of the TV, each dress like their favorite *Toy Story 2* characters, and eat food that made them think of the film. She spent two hours making a cake that looked like Hamm, the pig, then another hour cutting vegetables and chicken in chunks small enough for Oliver to eat, arranging them on a huge platter in the shape of the horse, Bullseye.

With straws and construction paper attached to the back of his footed pajamas, Oliver toddled around trying to fly like Buzz Lightyear, and Bea pinned orange yarn braids onto her faded straw hat. As in everything she did, Bea liked layering several details – even if she knew they weren't perfect - to create what she called "overall effect," something she said her mama taught her, which allowed her to cut herself some slack when something didn't quite pan out as she had hoped. Lloyd found it entertaining to witness out of the corner of his eye, but it seemed less important than surfing the Web at the time, so he remained detached from the festivities, piping in with occasional "uh-huhs" from the computer chair in the office and tapping his foot under the desk to Randy Newman. He pouted at Bea when she walked past to get a tissue. She always cried when Sarah McLachlan sang "When Somebody Loved Me" for Jessie the cowgirl and always belittled herself for it. Ultimately Lloyd was much more focused on whatever MSN.com candy-news was consuming him at the time. Movie Night continued without him that time, and the next, and so on. Soon it was too late to join in because they no longer lived under the same roof.

Lloyd realized there was no footage in Oliver's brain of movie nights together. Although Lloyd had been there physically when they began, he was more like a memento one remembers seeing as they walk through a room, a snapshot with smile from a trip to Six Flags. During movie nights, as many other nights, he was uninvolved, a passerby. That was the past he shared with Oliver and with Bea, a past where he played no character in *Toy Story*. At least he could build character now, which is why he began casting spells in earnest on the canned goods in Aisle 10. Fueled by Oliver's increasing hysterics, he flicked his wand at the canned tomatoes, commanding "Reducto!"

"Reducto!" he called, flourishing his right arm dramatically.

Oliver doubled over with laughter.

"Reducto! Pow! Reducto! Bam!" Lloyd commanded with all the seriousness he could muster, bringing both arms above his head with light saber sound effects for a final, Jedi-like punishing swoosh that could destroy the goods of the evil Wal-Mart Empire.

"Dad!!!"

Seeing Oliver staring wide eyed, Lloyd turned around. His wand had just grazed the top tier of stacked canned tomatoes. Time froze as they watched in awe, the cans wobbling ever-so-slightly before coming crashing down all around them. Oliver's mouth flew wide open in shock and when, instinctually, he turned to run, he barreled directly into Zoe who had just entered the aisle.

"Whoa! Whoa! Whoa!" Zoe placed her hand on top of his head and pivoted him back into the aisle. "Little Olly-Loll? Is that you being the loud cheeky monkey?" She said all this to Oliver, but she stared at Lloyd, who at this point had turned roma tomato red.

"It wasn't me! It was Dad!"

"Ahh, should've known. You can't take him anywhere, hey mate? So, Lloyd, I see you are doing as well as would be expected."

"Hi, Zoe. Heh heh. Yeah, I'm fine," Lloyd plastered on a smile as he worked rapidly to restock the shelf while Zoe ignored the mess, stepping over numerous dented cans to get what she needed from the shelves.

"What are you doing here, Zoe?" Oliver asked, clearly over his earlier flight response. "My dad and I are here going through his list. He made it on the computer and knows everything there is to know about the stuff in this store."

"Wow, who wouldn't be impressed with that?" she looked drolly at Lloyd. "I'm running errands. I offered to help your Mum get some ingredients for a lasagna she's making tonight." Then, in a quasi-whisper to Lloyd she said "for her date. His name is Sam, and I believe she would describe him as scrumptious and 'packing'. Oh, I mean, because he's an officer of the law and all." Zoe gave him an exaggerated wink.

"Cool. See ya," Oliver said as he climbed back into the cart to rehearse his "Reducto."

"Bye, Loll." Zoe paused briefly to scan the shelf. "Lloyd," she said to the air as she walked past.

"Yeah, goodbye Zoe," Lloyd smiled stiffly. He picked up the last can, then briskly wheeled the cart through the remainder of the list lost in his own thoughts.

Lasagna. That's a date-number-four meal for Bea. A great recipe. One of her favorites and a quick favorite of anyone else who gets to sample it. Warm, comforting, filling. Great with a whole bottle of red wine, good conversation, a long night. Just like Bea. Shit. I'm in trouble. Once any reasonable man gets a taste and realizes what's at stake, he'll pull out all the stops and make a big move. I've seen it happen a few times since the divorce: Keith, Ryan, Barry, and now Sam. Hell, it happened with me when we first met, and it happened with those bozos one per semester since the divorce has been official. It's Bea's intimacy preamble. Maybe she's lonely, Lloyd thought. *She wants to connect but she can't find a connection like ours. Bea uses that damn, comfort food recipe as a doorway to let someone in. And each time she lets one of those bastards in, she pulls further from me. It gets that much harder to find our way back together. I need a fucking plan. Now.*

Chapter 7

Bea sliced through her lasagna with Sam's crystal-handled pie server and handed him a piece. She had to admit, although his musical tastes may have been bound by rather claustrophobic borders, Sam had a broad and impressive collection of fine dinnerware. Wüsthof knives, crystal wine glasses, gold rimmed plates, and a beautiful spun glass vase that held flowers he had cut earlier in the day from his garden while she cooked.

Nice attention to detail, she thought. *Perhaps too nice...?* She silently chastised herself for seeking out flaws. *Well, he is a never-been-married nearing 40. What's with all the crystal ware, dude? What the hell has he been doing since we used to work together 10 years ago: becoming a Hummel figurine collector or something?* She imperceptibly shook her head to clear the queries as he raised his wine glass her way.

"The lasagna smells delicious, Bea. Thanks for bringing it over." He leaned in and gave her a warm, closed-mouth kiss, which, as usual, turned her brain off and her pelvis on. *That's one way to clear the cobwebs.*

"Here's to a great dinner…and a great year." Sam clinked his glass to hers and winked.

Bea took a large drink of pinot noir before digging in to her dinner.

"So, when's your next race?" she asked between bites.

"Mmm, Saturday morning," Sam responded, wiping his mouth. "The whole team is committed to sub-90 finishes, so we've been pushing it hard, but this week is basically a rest week, which is good. Really good, in fact, because it means I don't have to hop out of bed before the butt-crack of dawn every morning. I can sleep in. Then I can run behind you and comment on how good your caboose looks." He smiled at her, raising his eyebrows.

Bea shot him a shy smile and continued enjoying her lasagna. She'd never been able to decide if his antiquated phrases were endearing or annoying. *I mean, who says 'caboose', really?*

"Very pretty glassware," she said, swirling her next drink around and goading him slightly. "Which woman with great taste left these behind when she skedaddled?"

Sam looked momentarily flushed. "Bachelors can have good taste, too, you know. Unlucky in love, lucky in ornamentation." He brought his own glass to his lips and Bea could swear he gulped his next drink. What's that about? She stopped herself again.

"Well, they're beautiful regardless of how they arrived here," she smiled warmly at him and took a sip. At this Sam grabbed the arm of her chair and skidded her seat next to his while she giggled and tried not to spill her wine. He reached his hand gently behind her head, weaving his fingers into her hair, and pressed his lips to hers again. As he scooped her legs up with his other arm,

Bea had no doubt her visceral reaction was palpable from the next town over.

Harold moaned audibly as he bit through his chocolate, Bavarian-crème-filled breakfast. "Mmm. Uhh. Oh my God. I swear World's Fair Doughnuts laces their baking sheets with crack. Seriously," he said, with his mouth full and eyes closed.

Lloyd hadn't eaten anything from his bag yet. It was still folded just the same way it was handed to him, and it now sat untouched on his floorboard. He was razor-focused on the road, craning his neck to get the best angles from the front and side windows and squinting to maximize his field of vision. "Yeah," he mumbled distractedly as he held the keys still dangling from the ignition. "Are you finished yet? Cause we need to get going."

Harold burped and took a drink of Red Bull. "What difference does it make? We're, like, ten blocks from the basketball court, and you know we get our asses kicked *every* time because you still don't understand screen defense and couldn't hit a shot if your life depended on it. What's the rush, 'Minute' Bol?"

"We just need to do something first." Lloyd turned off the car and jumped out quickly. "C'mon. Let's go. Let's go."

"Okay, okay. For fuck's sake," Harold complained, rolling out of the passenger side and wiping icing off his face. "Where the hell are we going?" he yelled as Lloyd began to sprint. Lloyd simply reached an arm back and waved for Harold to follow as he continued running.

Lloyd cut behind one house, then another, then up the next cross street. His mind was focused only on two things: he knew he had to book it or he would miss her, and he knew he had to lose those extra twenty pounds and stop eating breakfast at World's Fair Doughnuts or suffer a massive heart attack within the next five years.

He could hear Harold's stream of expletives half a block back, and his own heartbeat pounded in his eardrums. Regardless, he knew he had to keep going. As he rounded the corner to Mason Road he did everything he could to look nonchalant and not as close to death as he felt. Like somehow he belonged there. Like he always jogged there. Like he always sucked in desperate gasps for breath when he jogged there.

Bea neared Mason at that moment. Lloyd slowed his pace to what he hoped was a believable time and watched her rounding the corner. Even though he was exhausted, he couldn't help but smile as he saw her briefly turn her face up to the sky enjoying the weather. She rotated her shoulders a few times to loosen her neck and made a barely perceptible "pump it up" gesture indicating she was enjoying the tunes piping in through her headphones. If he was a betting man, he would have said she was listening to Michael Franti's new album, or perhaps Al Green. He was pretty sure he had heard both of those wafting out of car the last few times they met to swap Oliver. It took her a few seconds to focus her eyes straight ahead again, and when she did, she smiled, thus convincing Lloyd the impending heart attack was worthwhile.

"Hey. You decide to take up jogging today?" Bea said

with a quizzical smile.

"Nah, I've been running lately." Lloyd stretched widely and jogged in place for a second, trying not to suck air like a fish out of water. "You know, for a while now. Just kicked up my speed today so I'm a little more out–, out of breath…than usual." He tried to act casual while resting his hand on the stitch under his right ribcage.

"Yeah, the endorphins kick ass. Glad you finally decided to get active. Great for your heart, and ultimately great for Oliver. See ya." Bea put her earbuds back in and ran around him. Lloyd tried to protest and searched for something, anything he could say to keep her there for a while longer. Anything. But the lack of oxygen choked off his words and his synapses, and instead he leaned over with his hands on his thighs gasping loudly.

As Lloyd watched her moving further and further away, Harold stumbled up, wheezing. Red-cheeked and still bearing chocolate around the corners of his mouth, he collapsed on the grass near Lloyd.

His repeated threat to kill Lloyd came out sounding more like he was whispering "IKEA" over and over.

"I thought... I thought for sure she'd stay to talk longer. She loves coming this way once the weather gets cooler. Puts her in such a good mood," Lloyd said, lunging to stretch his tightening quads.

"I ca-, I can't believe you, you-…just for this shit-….I'll ki-…you will pay." Harold was finally able to get the last words out before he was overtaken by a massive coughing fit.

Chapter 8

"So tell me again why No-Tongue Guy gets your panties in such a bunch. Does the no tongue only apply to above the waist, maybe?"

Bea spewed part of her vanilla soy latte across the Starbucks table at Zoe's comment. "Zoe! I'm not sure which is worse: that question, or the fact that you've named him No-Tongue Guy."

"He doesn't believe in French kissing, you don't believe in keeping secrets from me, neither of which is my fault. Regardless, Lovey, I just name 'em. You're the one who picks 'em." Zoe tapped her chin with her finger as she thought. "Let's see. There was The Politician... Daddy issues?" Zoe asked.

"Nah. Quite the hottie. However, his desire for a traveling trophy wife, as you can imagine, didn't make my syllabus."

"Then we had Clumsy Cowboy who, between riding horses and racing stock cars, managed to break every bone in his body. Including the bone he broke after four months in bed with you."

Bea blew into her mug and rolled her eyes.

"Top Gun! Whatever happened to him?"

"Hmm, yeah." Bea gazed off into the distance. "That, my friend, is a very long and lovely story, full of heartbreak and unfortunate circumstances. Synopsis? Great match; sucky timing.”

“Mmm. Of course, and we all remember the Comedian. I liked him. Bit of a sarcastic dick.”

“Yep. Too much like Howard Stern in all the best and worst ways.”

“After my own heart, really. Oh! And, who could forget Professor Dumblebutt?” Zoe said, a little quieter, as they were in a popular campus hangout. They both giggled.

“Yeah, who could forget the many lectures I sat through, incapable of offering up the appropriate mathematical proof to validate ‘I’m just not that into you,’ Whilst being both worshipped *and* chastised for being too ignorant to know what’s good for me. Super fun.” They both snickered. Bea paused, then joined the fun. “You forgot Backfro.”

“I do try to forget him, yes,” Zoe crinkled her nose in disgust. “I mean, that’s a lot of hair, mate. It’s not like we’re asking you to go and get a boyzilian. Just a little bit of personal grooming, you know? And, it’s particularly disappointing when you can’t see the wood for the forest. But, now it’s No-Tongue Guy who has you all randy.”

“Oh my God. Don’t even say that name. Remember Randy? He was *such* an asshole. He doesn’t even get the honor of a nickname.” Bea sipped her drink and shook off a chill.

“I guess my question, therefore, is this: Is No-Tongue Guy something special or just another float in the parade of four-date boy-toys?” Zoe asked.

Bea blushed a little and looked out the window. "He's hot. I mean, despite the no-tongue thing; he does it for me big time."

"Are you sure he actually has a tongue? I mean, have you ever seen it? Perhaps he's a mutant created in a lab or something. It makes sense; cause, you know, who really has a body like that anyway? He's like the Bionic Man or something. I don't know, Lovey. Perhaps he can't kiss with an open mouth or your saliva will short circuit his central processing unit. I'd ask to see his birth certificate to be honest with you. Of course, anything can be faked nowadays. Even your rand-, your level of interest in his tongueless boudoir." Zoe winked, grabbed her Sailor Moon backpack, and stood to go. "What you didn't say, though, is if he does any more for you than rev your engine, Lovey. I think that's the better question."

Bea just took a sip and stared back at Zoe.

Zoe winked. "Ta for the drink. I'll see you at trivia tonight."

Waving over her mug, Bea watched Zoe leave. She promptly picked up her stack of midterm papers in hopes that she could get another ten essays graded, but she soon put them down. Her mind was racing over questions, considerations, expectations, and, as the French say, *baisant.*

Lloyd did his best to tune in to Oliver's jabber through dinner, and to be in the moment while playing Yahtzee. He even managed to coax Oliver through a typical "I'm-not-winning-so-this-game-is-stupid" mini-tantrum. After Oliver went to bed, Lloyd even got enjoyment out of lying across the couch watching George Lucas share his genius in *The Empire of Dreams,* but he was never fully present mentally. Rather, he was drawing up relationship offense, strategizing, and thinking about Bea smiling over trivia at The Replay tonight.

For the last few weeks, he had spent an inordinate amount of time thinking of strengths he could use to his advantage. What was it that Bea said to him once? It was hot for April and she was waving early mosquitos away from her face and quoting literature to him from the grill. Multitasking, as always, she was studying for her Thursday night grad class and cooking steaks. "Victory can be achieved if the warrior is formless," she said, or something like that. Lloyd wished he could remember specifically. He wasn't a reader, per se, a factoid he cemented mid-relationship to an appalled Bea when he proudly confessed that he had somehow made it through his entire undergraduate degree without reading one single book cover-to-cover. She had been horrified, and, truth be told, he was convinced she never looked at him quite the same way after that.

But he was fairly certain that was how the quote went, and he had a pretty good memory. He was reasonably confident it had come from *The Art of War,* which seemed appropriate, since he was fighting tooth and nail to rebuild this relationship.

Ultimate strategy, that's what I need. If I'm going to be victorious, I'm going to need one kickass strategy; covert enough that I can remain "formless," but effective enough in its design to render me victorious. Since I am not actually Sun Tzu, however, (or George Lucas, for that matter, and I should seriously turn the TV off before I go to my room and pull out my light saber), I am at a clear disadvantage.

What do I have going for me? A strong will, proven by my collection of Star Wars toys still in their packaging, and a reputation for being the Lord of Worthless Minutiae. I'm the person who can remember the name of the theme song to "The Greatest American Hero," how many Oscar nominations Oliver Stone has (or hasn't) received, and who was on the cover of the first TV Guide. I'm the person Bea wants on her trivia team, without question, but not currently the person she wants in her bed, despite my attempts to convince her otherwise. I'm the master of the popcorn canon. Go me.

Lloyd paused and rubbed his face. *Oh yeah. Why she isn't breaking down my door right now, I'll never know.* He turned off the TV, pinching the bridge of his nose as he fell back into the couch and closed his eyes.

He didn't hear the door open, but he thought he heard it close, so he immediately jerked upright and opened his eyes, hands up like a Ninja who forgot his martial arts training. He looked around, squeezed his eyes open and shut several times, and looked again. John Cusack. John Cusack was in his living room. John Cusack was in his living room in a trench coat. John Cusack was in his living room in a trench coat, pacing.

"Lloyd, Lloyd. Look, you're Lloyd, I'm Lloyd. I don't know. All I can tell you is, I'm here and you're here and you just-, the way you-" he held his temples, "you're just-" He sighed, "it's going to take everything we've got for a girl like this, you know? It's, she's- … look, I don't want to do anything to scare you or stop you or stop scaring you or…will you just, just come outside for a second? Okay?"

Lloyd was so taken aback by John Cusack's presence pacing up and down in front of his front door that he didn't question it at all. He just went with it, stood up, and followed him outside. As he was stepping out and pulling the door behind him, however, he immediately noticed three things. First, his front porch was gone, replaced by a street-level parking lot. Second, Harold was sitting on a curb in that lot and there was a Gas-N-Sip where his apartment used to be. Third, he could feel the temperature dropping even through the tan trench coat he was suddenly wearing. Lloyd and John Cusack paced in unison in front of Harold as he sat on a parking bump outside the Gas-N-Sip plowing through a bag of Funyons and a Miller Lite.

"Look," Harold said through a mouthful. "All you gotta do is find a girl that looks just like her, fuck her, and then dump her, man." He paused, smiled, then shoved another Funyon in his mouth. "God, I love that line."

"Actually, it's 'nail her.' Cameron Crowe had to limit the number of f-bombs in order to avoid the R rating," Lloyd corrected. Cusack nodded vigorously beside him as they continued to pace together.

"Whatever. All I'm saying is you just need to get over her. Forget her, man. Look at me. No worries, no responsibilities, no stress."

Lloyd continued pacing, his movements synced with Cusack's in lockstep. "No family, no future, no thanks."

John chimed in. "Yeah. Lloyd doesn't care if he gets the shit kicked out of him. He wants to give her his whole heart." They paced identically.

Harold looked between the two, shook his head, and tossed his empty Funyons bag into the parking lot. "Wait, what am I supposed to say here? Oh yeah, you give her your heart, she'll give you a pen, or some shit like that. Then, you can use it to write in your Care Bears diary like a 12-year-old girl."

"Look, Harold, I have no idea why this is happening or why my brain or subconscious or a different dimension decided to place me smack in the middle of *Say Anything*. Maybe I had too many chips with salsa while I was cooking dinner. Who knows? All I know is when it comes to Bea, I'm totally and completely serious. I don't want to date anyone else, instant message anyone else, or sleep with anyone else, or sleep with anyone through messaging or date anyone who's sleeping or whatever. All I want is to hang out with Bea."

"That's it," John Cusack echoed over his shoulder. "All he wants. He's gonna call her. He's totally and completely serious."

Harold just shook his head as he brushed Funyon crumbs off his knees. "It's your choice, man. Just a heads up, though: you can only rarely find functional boom boxes at Goodwill at this point, and your ass is so old you'll probably end up in traction if you decide to hold it over your head for an entire Peter Gabriel song. I seriously hope you didn't pay much for that trench coat just because someone on eBay said it was 'authentic from the movie set,'" Harold said as he cracked open another beer and stretched his legs.

Lloyd stopped pacing and stood in front of him. "Harold, if you know so much about women, why are you sitting outside the Gas-N-Sip alone on a Saturday, no women in sight, eating Funyons?"

Harold paused. "By choice. I just got my car detailed. I don't need any crumbs in there." He wadded up the bag and threw it at Lloyd.

Lloyd awoke with a gasp just as the bag sailed towards his face. His DVD player told him it was 2:03AM. He sat up from the couch and blinked a few times. Then, slowly, he broke into a huge smile.

Chapter 9

"So, tell me again why John Cusack was in St. Louis last night?"

Lloyd shook his head but maintained his excitement. "I didn't say he was necessarily *in* St. Louis, just that I saw him in my living room."

Harold used the ends of his chopsticks to stab two pieces of sushi and shove them, one after the other, into his mouth, pausing only for a breath before he responded, "If John Cusack was in St. Louis, he'd go to Schlafly's, or Tower Grove, or hell, even a Cardinals game. That shit would have been plastered all over the Riverfront Times. You can't seriously expect me to believe he flew under the radar and went to your house." He paused to take a quick sip of his green tea, his pinky extended, then went back to stabbing sushi. "Unless of course you're telling me he went there with every intention of going all *Gross Pointe Blank* on your ass, and in that case, please tell me more."

"I am totally and completely serious! I mean, at least in that I saw him in my house, like fresh from my subconscious or something. Maybe a rerun of one of his movies was playing on Showtime when I was falling asleep, or maybe because I know it's one of Bea's favorite movies. Who knows? All I know is it was destiny. Pure and simple. It's like, once I jumped into the experience and let go of all the frustrations, I didn't question it. It just made perfect sense. The path was clear. I slept, all my normal thoughts went away, and there it was. The way to Bea."

Harold stabbed the thicker end of his chopstick into the next piece of sushi and shoved it into his mouth. "You're right about all the normal going away. That's for damn sure."

"What?!? Haven't you ever figured something out because you saw or did something that set off a trigger? Like, don't you ever have a dream or hear a song or see a movie and think, 'Hey! That's it. That's the answer. That's what I should do!?'"

Harold pondered a second, chewing. "You mean like when I watched *Rambo II* and suddenly realized we actually won Vietnam? Or, oh yeah, like when I listened to Jack White's 'Seven Nation Army' for the first time and I knew exactly what I needed to do to pull in $5 million a year? Oh, yeah. Happens all the time." Harold rolled his eyes.

Lloyd's enthusiasm couldn't be hampered, "So in this dream I was talking to you in the Gas-N-Sip parking lot, which somehow appeared outside my house. You were Jeremy Piven and I was John Cusack…well, and John Cusack was John Cusack, too. You were giving me crappy advice, which, to be fair, was both realistic and verbatim from the scene, and I was channeling Lloyd Dobler, trying to find a way to reach the love of my life. It's really logical. It actually makes sense when you think about it. What's my ultimate strength in life?"

"Let's see, I know this one. Your super power? I got it. Your power to become a bucket of sweat simply by walking from your cubical to mine, Wonder Twin?"

"No," Lloyd said.

"Your magical high-salary shield that enables you to make $10,000 a year less than our sushi server, despite a double major from a top ten business school?"

Lloyd glowered.

"I got it! I got it! Your ability to leap to illogical conclusions in a single bound?"

Lloyd cocked his head and looked at Harold with burgeoning irritation. "You know as well as I do what I rock at. I kick ass at trivia, particularly entertainment trivia. I'm the Lord of Movie Minutiae. Hands down, I am always the most successful player around."

"And that means what?"

"What's something Bea loves?"

"To torment you, apparently."

"She doesn't torment me. Well, I mean, she does, but she doesn't intentionally. She just hasn't realized yet how much better we are together. Anyway, what Bea loves is movies, pop culture. She even has a movie theatre in her house, for Christ's sake! She studies media for a living, man! It's like a match made in heaven," Lloyd said, momentarily staring out the window.

"Again, I ask: So?"

"So pop culture is her thing; it's at the core of who she is. And I've got the power of pop culture behind me, dude! Unlike some, I *do* know jack! No one knows movies like I do," Lloyd's voice lowered as he leaned in with a grin. "And I especially know what Bea loves to love, particularly when it comes to movies."

Harold picked up the menu. "Are you going to make a point soon, or should I just go ahead and ask the waitress to bring me another order and you the check?"

"My point is, even if *I've* been unable to reach her heart, I know the entertainment that can. I've seen how emotional movies and songs and stuff make her. They're a direct line to the Secret Garden of her heart, man!"

Lloyd leaned toward Harold, smiling. Harold leaned back toward him, eyebrows raised and silent. After a couple of seconds Harold shrugged and shook his head to indicate he still didn't get it.

"So, follow me here, if I can get her to feel the way she feels while experiencing those things that mean so much to her, I'm golden! I'm in like Flynn, baby! If I can draw that intense emotion out, and she attributes it to me, we're back, and I think I know exactly how to do it."

"This should be good. Hold on a sec. I'm just gonna hit record on my phone to capture this moment. Oh, and then later I'll create what the kids today call a 'mashup' with this and the D-Day scene in *Saving Private Ryan.* Go on. This should be good."

Lloyd briefly glared at him, but he was still running high. "It's simple. All I have to do is to channel the scenes and lines I know she loves. Reminiscent but not an exact replica, you know? Something close that will draw out those feelings. You get me? I know movies and music, and I definitely know the movies and music Bea knows and loves. It should be easy…well, at least easy to target the right places. To pull it off, though, I'll need to be selective. I mean, there's no easy way for me to act out something with an ensemble cast of, say, the *Love Actually* variety, unless I hire a flash mob or something, so those favorites are no-goes."

"Oh, I don't know about that," Harold said. "I think you might have enough people talking in your head that you could make that happen."

Lloyd ignored him. "And I'll only want to choose story lines in the happily-ever-after realm. That'll be key. These will need to be Bea-classics, and they'll have to be easily recognizable. This way I can simulate enough of the original shock and awe, draw out a sufficient amount of that ingrained romantic feeling lying within Bea, for it to be successful. She'll realize how much attention I paid, how much work I put in, how I think all the same things are romantic and enchanting, and she'll want to pick up where we left off." Lloyd grinned, sat back, and waited for Harold to acknowledge his sheer brilliance.

Harold paused then looked around incredulously at the nearby business-lunchers enjoying their sashimi as if they would jump in to help prove his point. "You've thought about this quite a bit."

Lloyd nodded, grinning.

Harold paused, took a drink, shoved a giant piece of spicy tuna roll into his mouth, and continued. "That is, by far, the stupidest thing you've said since last year when you said 'I'm going on an all fruit diet' and then almost shit your pants walking through Walmart. You've completely lost it, dude," he said and stabbed another bite.

"It will work. Trust me."

"I'll tell you what," Harold said with a mouthful while he indicated to the server that Lloyd wanted the check. "If you succeed in pulling off this Looney Tunes stunt, I will personally pay for a second honeymoon for you and Bea, which is a safe bet to never happen." He paused to wipe his mouth. "Hell, even if it did, it would make zero impact on my wallet, because you're afraid to fly anywhere."

"Done. Get ready to shell out big time, my friend."

"Hold your horses, Pal. That was a big *if.* Because if you fail to win Bea back, and I've wagered my fair share, you're gonna have to match the pot."

Lloyd slammed his palm on the table. "Done. I'm in. That's how confident I am. Name your price."

"Don't get too cocky, Wile E. Coyote. You've got a lot of strings to pull to make that Acme plot actually pan out." Harold looked at the waitress staring at their table and motioned for the check. "I'll tell you what's at stake. I'll give you until May to win her back, which will be the end of her school year and this crazy concept schooling you. If you haven't won her back by May, I'm signing you up for the Glo Run – yeah, you know, the one where all the freaks wear costumes and makeup and shit while they sweat like crazy and run for miles, and you have to wear whatever I tell you to while you run the entire race. That's right, Fucker. I told you I'd get you back for that unplanned run the other day."

Lloyd didn't pause. "No problem, because there's no way I can fail."

Harold stood, wiped his mouth, and tossed his napkin toward Lloyd. "We'll see. Now let's get out of here before you decide your next dumbass move is implanting a butt-chin to make you look more like Aaron Eckhart or John Travolta."

Back at work Lloyd did just enough of his tasks to remain employed, then spent the rest of his day gazing off wearing his headphones while making a list of possible movies he could dive into that still fell within his predefined parameters. He eliminated *Once, The Philadelphia Story,* and *500 Days of Summer* because, although they were some of Bea's favorites, the characters didn't end up together. He also nixed *Juno* and *Harold and Maude,* because he didn't want anyone to die or divorce. As his mind raced through the movie catalog, he realized he was rapidly tapping his pencil to the beat of "Rose Rouge" on Pandora and he froze. *That's it,* he thought. *This can't be coincidence. This song, Jeremy Piven, John Cusack. No way that's a coincidence. It's serendipity.* He purchased the song for inspiration and played it on repeat while shutting down his workspace for the day.

Bea had their only copy of the movie, so he racked his brain for a place to rent it. Netflix? No streaming version available. Blockbuster? Closed. Redbox? Too old. A brief search revealed only one option: the public library. *Easy. Run in, open an account, grab the movie, and I'm out in time to pick up fast food, plop in front of the TV, and watch it a few times before bed.* That was the plan. He threw his remaining paperwork into his in-tray and raced out the lobby door on a mission, music blasting in his ears.

Chapter 10

Despite loving parties and people, especially fall parties with fire pits and sweaters, warm drinks and crisp air, Bea couldn't quite get comfortable,. She smiled and chatted with her colleagues and their partners and regularly placed her hand on Sam's arm anytime he offered to get her another drink or refill her plate, but she was antsy and restless, keeping busy like someone anticipating severe weather but knowing the storm wouldn't hit for another few hours.

To distract herself, she went down to the basement to watch Zoe own the crowd at epic Xbox Karaoke Revolution. After laughing with the room as Zoe belted out a spectacularly off-key version of "Wind Beneath My Wings," she looked up and noticed Sam poking his head in the downstairs doorway. He caught her attention and winked. She smiled back warmly and headed toward the steps to rejoin him, all the while feeling Professor Dumblebutt's glare radiate through her body as it attempted to incinerate Sam. Rather than head back into the dining room, Sam grabbed her hand and led her through the backdoor to chat by the patio heaters.

"Interesting people," Sam smiled.

"Yeah, sorry," Bea said, apologetically. "Academics. They're a different breed, aren't they? Are you beyond bored?"

"Nah, never when I'm with you," Sam warmly kissed her cheek. "You're cold." He squeezed her shoulder. "Do you want to go back inside?"

"No, no, this is nice," Bea said, hugging herself and giving her arms a brief rub as they stood side-by-side in front of the stainless patio heater. "Please tell me Dr. Ebernich didn't force you to listen to key points from his latest blog posting on the Anthropic Principle while you ate your spinach dip."

"I couldn't tell you. I was half listening while trying to reload my plate with cocktail shrimp before he could inhale them all. Big guy, big ideas," Sam finished off the last of his beer and turned to face Bea. "Thanks for inviting me. I'd much prefer to be with you rather than at home on a Saturday night wondering who's bringing you drinks at your work party."

"Me too. I'm glad you're here. Want another beer?"

"Sure, but first I want to ask you something. How attached are you to your house?"

Bea raised her eyebrows and froze. "Why? Are you in the market for a new place?" she laughed nervously.

"Mmm... maybe. I was thinking about it sometime after we get through the holiday hoopla, but only if you're in it with me. You and Oliver."

Bea's lips parted slightly but no sound followed.

"Look," Sam said, "you know we love spending time together, and we're not getting any younger..."

"Speak for yourself," Bea retorted.

"...and I think we should spend more time together. Your place, my place. We both have three bedrooms and two-car garages. We each live equi-distance from the university in either direction. What do you think?"

Bea chugged the last few sips of her beer and let out a quick breath. "Wow, I think you've been thinking a lot for someone focused on scarfing down shrimp. How long have you been thinking about this?"

"If I said 'since we reconnected at The Ballroom', which was like four months ago, would that terrify you?" Sam smiled and put his hands on her waist and continued before she could respond. "Look. We've known each other for years. We know we are great together. Why not learn the rest together? What do you say?"

"Ummm, I say…let's talk more about this after the party, okay?" Bea briefly touched his arm and turned to head back inside for more beer. In her agitated state, however, she miscalculated the height of her boot heels and tripped up the steps, gracefully sprawling face-first onto the linoleum in front of the guests gathered in the kitchen and ripping a huge hole in her pants. Everyone came to the rescue, a few applauded, and she self-consciously took a bow and laughed at herself while Sam helped bandage her knee.

"How about I get the drinks?" Sam said, touching her face.

How about another five drinks? She tried to mentally attribute the need for the alcohol to her throbbing knee and the accompanying pain and embarrassment, but in reality she knew she just wanted to be too plastered to talk through Sam's idea after the party.

Lloyd knew Oliver would wake up by 7 o'clock, which gave him just enough time to watch *Serendipity* once more before he absolutely had to go to bed or he'd be too exhausted to interact at breakfast. This would be the seventh time this weekend (the last seventh time being illegitimate, as he fell asleep 27 minutes in) he was watching the movie for inspiration, but he knew the right approach would reveal itself at some point. He had already determined filling her living room full of rose petals was out of the question. He no longer had a key, and unless he could somehow fill a trash bag full of petals and air, slide the opening under her door, stomp, and run away before she opened it and saw him, she'd know who did it and would be none too happy. That one would be hard to pin on a Halloween prankster if she got angry. She probably also would not enjoy cleaning up the mess.

He contemplated leaving her nested, wrapped boxes containing a piece of jewelry, but he thought that was too close to the actual scene. Sliding a plane ticket under her face while she got one of her monthly massages was also out; based on previous experience, he knew the front desk staff at Massage Haven would stop him before he reached her. Committed to finding just the right approach, he clicked "Play" once more. He *was* committed, convinced the time for their reunion had come. He searched the movie for little clues he could draw on to build a plan, like random bits of lint off a sweater brought together purposefully, lovingly, in the hopes uniting them might reveal what Jonathan Trager's best friend, Dean Kansky, in *Serendipity* described as a "tapestry." And he was convinced that plan would help him win the woman for whom he was destined.

But he always got frustrated during the sweet shop scene in *Serendipity*. Each time he watched the two main characters – John Cusack and Kate Beckinsale - eat ice cream he got hungry, and after about viewing number four he had to switch from jeans to sweat pants. Now, the seventh time around, he grumbled as he walked to the kitchen for the chips and salsa. He sat the salsa bowl down too vigorously on the coffee table and ended up splashing chunks of it onto the birthday card his mother sent. Lloyd disliked the card, as he usually disliked cards his mother sent him, so he was somewhat pleased it gave him an excuse to throw it away. Her cards usually had cars or bears or trains on them, as if he was perpetually turning five in her mind. This one had been particularly heinous, the worst of all worlds: a fluffy bear holding what appeared to be an iPad with a reflective screen facing the reader above a caption reading "You're the apple of my i." *Horrendous.*

As he walked with it to the trash can and headed back toward the TV he suddenly remembered a card Bea gave him when they were dating and he chuckled to himself. On the front was a sexy woman dressed like a schoolgirl and holding an apple. He couldn't remember precisely what she'd written inside, but he remembered her razzing him about it. Throughout their marriage, she teased him regularly about not reading what she wrote (in cards, in journals, on to-do lists) and generally not being interested in what she had to say. It became a sore spot in their relationship, eventually. In actuality he kept every note and card she gave him and never mentioned it. They were all in a manila "Bea" envelope in his nightstand. He made a mental note to look at the schoolgirl card again before he went to sleep.

Lloyd put a chipful of dip in his mouth when he sat back down and watched Kate Beckinsale write her name and number in the front of a Gabriel Garcia Marquez novel, a pivotal scene in *Serendipity,* and that's when it hit him. He had found the treasure.

Lloyd raced to his bedroom, opened his nightstand to grab the envelope, and dumped its contents onto his bed. A quick sift and he found the card. Inside, Bea had written "You've taught me everything I know about love. What we learn together from here is limitless." He knew she'd never remember verbatim what she had written in that card. That was years and many dissertation chapters ago, but, he knew the words would resonate. He also knew without a doubt he'd have to write it inside a copy of *Love in the Time of Cholera.*

What he didn't immediately know was where to leave the book. In her car was too obvious. Selling it at the university's used book store and hoping she found it was too risky. He didn't want to wait years for their relationship to kick-start. If there's one thing *Serendipity* taught everyone, it's that although you may be destined to be together, it may take you a long-ass time to reconnect if you take stupid chances. No, it had to be findable fast.

Lloyd was convinced somewhere at the university would be key and remembered he was supposed to take Oliver to Bea Tuesday night just after her evening class concluded. That was it. He and Oliver would simply arrive fifteen minutes early and head to her office, which he knew she kept unlocked so students could always drop assignments off. He also knew Bea stayed after lectures to talk with students, especially her evening students, as she knew it might be the only course many of them could take and still juggle daytime jobs. It was her favorite part of the day. That would give Lloyd the time he needed to drop the book on her desk and perhaps mix it up a bit in her piles of work so she'd stumble upon it. *Genius,* he thought, and smiled as he walked back to turn off the TV.

"Thanks, Evan. So next week you'll do your presentation for my students from 6-7, then we'll have Q&A. Sound good? Okay, see you then. Take care." Bea hung up smiling.

Evan was an animal rights guest lecturer she invited to speak each semester to the students in her persuasion course. Controversial, loved, and hated, she enjoyed how passionate he was about what he did, and although she didn't agree with everything he touted, she admired his enthusiasm. In fact, she wished she was brave enough to take the leap and pursue her passion full time without fearing any consequences. *Writing full-time, every day.* Just the thought of it made her smile, and cringe.

Writing, just writing in several genres full-time would mean pursuing what burned in the core of her being, as well as opening herself up for sometimes-brutal criticism. Criticism that wasn't rooted in polite academic debate. She had swallowed that in doses since grad school. That kind of criticism felt removed, as she was typically testing others' theories of others utilizing a somewhat-formulaic approach to academic content creation. But writing for any genre, writing poetry and fiction, writing about ideas originating from within her, drawing an explicit picture for others as to what it was really like inside Bea. That thought left her excited and terrified. Certainly, too terrified to act on it.

Bea opened her mail lost in thought: an envelope containing an extra copy of an oral history primer she could place on reserve at the library, an invoice to submit for the western conference, and her copy of the *Journal of Gender Studies*. Her mind drifted to tenure requirements and what it might be like to write for a year with no interruptions. *Hell, to have three months with Oliver in a small cottage near a lake somewhere in Italy or a cabin far up in the Rockies. Even better if my parents or Lloyd took Oliver half of that time. Perhaps easiest in Hong Kong where the 85 decibels surrounding me in any establishment or courtyard would truly be white noise since I don't speak the language, a stream of light sound that wouldn't interrupt thoughts I don't have time to pursue. Unimaginable. So far from reality it feels painful.* She spread her mail neatly across her desk (journal, invoice, book in envelope) and closed her eyes, working hard to clear her mind before class began. Standing up, she took a deep breath, grabbed her book bag, and pulled the door closed behind her.

Lloyd couldn't help it. The theme from *Mission Impossible* could not be stifled in his head as he crept through the hallways with Oliver. He tried to keep Oliver as quiet as possible by giving him a Tootsie Pop and the "How many licks?" question right before heading into the Communications Building, and it worked like a charm. Oliver busily sucked away and counted licks towards the center as Lloyd led him toward Bea's office. About 20 feet away from the door he heard Zoe exchanging sexual jabs with someone from Sociology. Knowing she was nearby and could wrap up her harassment at any moment, he knew he had precious few minutes to carry out his plan.

This is it, he thought. *Open the door, place the book on her desk or shelf, and be back by her classroom door as she wrapped things up with the students.*

As he reached the office door he grabbed the handle, paused briefly, and twisted. The door opened easily. Oliver instinctively sat in Bea's office chair and spun in circles while Lloyd's eyes scanned the room quickly. In the dark of the office he noticed several items on her desk, including a manila envelope she had apparently just opened. Inside was some sort of oral history book, and based on the ripped envelope piece still lying next to it, as well as the postage date, she had just received it. Feeling safe that she'd flip through it tonight in her pajamas, Lloyd quickly slid the book out and put it under a stack of papers on her desk. Then, he slid his copy of *Love in the Time of Cholera* into the envelope.

He quickly turned to Oliver. "Well, she's not here. Let's go find Mommy." Lloyd pulled him by the hand, closed the door behind them, and headed toward the stairs.

Chapter 11

"I'm sorry, Dr. Stanley. Please educate me. Why again was this young lady screaming outside your office?"

"Dean Powell, as I stated earlier, she's under the mistaken assumption that I have some sort of inappropriate relationship with her boyfriend." Bea rubbed her forehead and glanced at the man next to the young woman in question who kept getting punched in the leg by the young woman while she shot daggers in Bea's direction, barely able to withhold a string of obscenities.

"And, young lady-"

"It's Megan," the young woman interrupted the dean.

"Megan, my dear, through what inductive line of reasoning did you reach the conclusion that Dr. Stanley here is having a, um... ahem, a relationship of sorts with your young man?" Dean Powell made his displeasure at spending a Thursday morning like this apparent to all in his office.

"I don't know what her reason is for going after Aaron. She's old, and she's, like, the teacher. Gross," Megan replied with visible nausea.

"I told you, Babe, there's nothing happening. It's all

a misunderstanding," Aaron said, then proceeded to lean behind Meghan's back to look across at Bea and whispered "'Sup "as he waggled his eyebrows.

Bea rolled her eyes, "Sir, apparently the confusion stems from the fact that there was a note written in the inside cover of a book Aaron borrowed."

Bea then recapped the previous night's events to the best of her ability. After Lloyd had dropped Oliver at her classroom at the end of the lecture, Bea took Oliver upstairs to drop off her materials. One of the other students, Lindsey, had accompanied her there and was asking for an editor's eye on an upcoming paper.

"I'd be happy to take a look at your draft, Lindsey, but I have to take my son home. Just email it or Dropbox it to me, okay? Thanks." She noted the shadow of another figure standing behind Lindsey. "Is he with you? Oh, hi, Aaron. I guess that just leaves you. What can I do for you?"

"Hey, yeah, thanks. So I was wondering how, like, set in stone the due dates on stuff were."

"Uh, well, whatever's in the syllabus, Aaron, is what we go by. That's why we have a syllabus," she told him as she threw stacks of papers into her satchel.

"Oh, okay. So here's the thing: I haven't gotten all of my student loan money yet, 'cause I filed late, so I haven't, like…actually…*purchased* the book yet that we need for our Barnhart project…" his voice went up sheepishly, and he squinted towards her.

Bea raised her eyebrows. "Aaron! What the…? Why didn't you tell me earlier? That way at least I could have lent you mine to make copies. Now you've missed two reflections and you'll have to really rock the essay quickly in order to pass this class at all." She sighed at Aaron's pleading face.

Every year, she and her students documented the stories of women at the local Barnhart textile plant. These women, many of whom were second generation employees from low income families, shared their experiences and those of the women who preceded them. Bea and her students documented these oral histories for posterity through a state grant-funded project. Bea loved the experience, and she was convinced the students got a lot out of it, at least those who actually bothered to read the material and do their assignments.

"Look, I just got another used copy this afternoon in the mail and was about to send it to the library reserves desk," she grabbed the opened FedEx envelope and handed it to him. "Photocopy a few sections to get started, do the last reflection, then drop that all off at my inbox tomorrow and we'll call it even, okay? Then you'll either have to duke it out with everyone else at the library to read this reserved copy, which I don't recommend, or buy your own copy."

"Awesome. Thanks a lot," Aaron said.

"C'mon, little man," Bea said to Oliver. "Let's go home. Stairs or elevator. Your choice."

Here's where things got a little hazy. Apparently later that evening Aaron's girlfriend Megan stumbled across that envelope, which, of course, sported Bea's name. Curious, she had opened it and found *Love in the Time of Cholera* inside. This had only increased her curiosity, as she had just read the SparkNotes for it in preparation for her gender studies class assignment and remembered it was described as a book about obsession. She then picked up the book, read a note written on the inside cover, and exploded with the veracity of two meerkats fighting over a queen ant. No one in the Dean's office could say precisely what was written on the page; Aaron's roommates only reported that Megan screeched, dropped several words no one was willing to share in the Dean's presence, ripped the page out, wadded it up, and set fire to it on Aaron's coffee table. When pointedly asked, Megan's only comment was, "it was just some gross, creepy teacher shit clearly designed to get Aaron in bed…ew."

Bea gave a quick "this is ridiculous" look to the Dean and took the FedEx packaging out of Aaron's hand. "Sir, I don't know why Used.com would have sent me the wrong text in the envelope. In fact, I'm absolutely convinced I saw the correct text when I glanced quickly before class. Nonetheless, all I can tell you is that I opened it yesterday before class and never took it out of the envelope. See the date? I was absolutely certain it contained the oral history primer when I handed the envelope to Aaron. Whether I simply thought I saw something different inside or accidentally grabbed the wrong envelope for him off my desk, this was all obviously an unfortunate misunderstanding. As you obviously know sometimes used books have notes written in the margins. Regardless, I had no motive for providing Aaron access to the wrong book, and I certainly have no illicit designs on him."

"Well," Dean Powell smiled and stood up, ushering

the group to his door, "sounds like the crisis has been averted. Young lady, perhaps you might consider providing your boyfriend, as well as Dr. Stanley, with a heartfelt apology on the way out."

"Yeah, good luck with that," Megan punched Aaron's arm hard as they stood to leave. "I'm sure he did *something* to deserve my outrage." She then turned to Bea, clucked her tongue, and snarled. "I can't believe *you* have four chili peppers on Rate My Prof. As if, Dr. Bea-otch." She stormed down the hallway.

Aaron shuffled after her, rubbing his arm. "Babe, c'mon," he said pleadingly, then walked backwards, briefly looking again toward Bea. "'Sup," he mouthed again and raised his eyebrows. Bea looked apologetically toward the Dean, who said nothing, but shooed her away with his hand. She rolled her eyes and quickly walked out of his office.

Lloyd was caught by surprise standing in the library's self-checkout queue when he heard, "Hey, Rom-Com Guy." The librarian grinned teasingly, approaching him from behind with a stack of books. "Enjoy watching *Serendipity* so much you're back for more young Mr. Cusack?"

"Absolutely. I mean, yes to the enjoyment, no to the more Cusack." He smiled broadly.

"Did she enjoy it, though? That's the real question. Well, or he. Either way."

"Who?"

"The love of your life, with whom I'm sure you watched it, of course."

"Uh, sure. Well, no. It's complicated." Lloyd stammered.

"Apparently," the librarian chuckled and held out her hand for his card.

"Oh, crap. I forgot my card back at my apartment. I'm not used to carrying it."

"Apparently not used to reading either. Who goes to the library with no library card?" she grinned. "It's okay. I can look you up. Name?"

"Lloyd. Stanley."

"Okay. Lloyd Stanley. Like Stan Lee. On 50th Street? For real, Spiderman?"

"Wow. Yep, that's me," Lloyd grinned, quite amazed and pleasantly shocked that she knew Marvel Comics headquarters was on 50th street. "And you are?"

"Handing you your movie now," she winked. "Have fun doing, well, whatever it is you're doing."

"Thanks. See you soon. Keep a hold on the Rom-Coms for me," Lloyd winked back, pointing his finger like triggering a gun.

Oh my God, Lloyd thought as he walked quickly through the cold night air. *It's not like me to do something so blatantly stupid and cheesy. Way to be cool, Loser, but, even that won't keep me from being in a good mood tonight. The book was delivered. The eagle has landed. Mission accomplished. Of course, I don't know how long it will take her to actually find the message written inside much less decode it and connect it to me. It's best, therefore, to move on to plan number two.*

Minutes in, even before his frustration could build

upon not hearing anything from Bea by, say, 10pm that evening, he decided to push forward in creating his next message by revisiting his "Bea movie list" and developing the next plan of attack.

It would have to be *Garden State*. One of her favorites. There was a lot to choose from there. Beautiful antique necklace, or wallpaper shirt? You can't go wrong with either. Shoplifted goods, or XTC? Let's pass on both. He already felt invigorated, as he knew this one almost as well as he knew the works of Stan Lee, and he felt confident he'd be graced by an epiphany with only one viewing. Lloyd grinned as he remembered the librarian. *Funny that she would reference Spiderman. Very few people know Marvel well enough to crack such a fabulously insider reference.* The car behind him honked, and Lloyd realized he had spaced out at the stoplight thinking about it. He quickly shook his head and turned toward home.

Zoe stopped to turn up Xavier Rudd on her stereo and danced back toward the couch to hand Bea her hot chocolate, all while doing her best vocal didgeridoo imitation. The complexity of this feat was amplified by the fact that she neither spilled her drink nor lost her toe separators.

"Did you go to the nail salon before I got here?" Bea asked looking down, confused by Zoe's unpainted toes.

"Nah, I just like the way these little thingies feel, you know? Like a squishy marshmallow man is holding hands with my toes." Zoe delicately propped her feet up on the pillow in Bea's lap as she continued bopping her head to the music. "Aww, that reminds me. I need to call my Mum."

"Does your Mum listen to Xavier Rudd?"

"Nah, the last time she rang me, though, I had gotten stoned and didn't hear her call because I was blasting *Food in the Belly* for three hours straight," Zoe grinned. "Now, let's talk about the real issue at hand, missy. What is this business again with NTG? He wants to calculate your home deduction or something?"

"No! You do remember he's not an accountant, right? And apparently you've now demoted him from 'No Tongue Guy' to just NTG? C'mon, he's at least worthy of a full nickname, isn't he? He's not that dull." Bea paused. "Is he?"

Zoe stared silently over her mug. "If you have to ask that, lovey, he must still not be doing much for you in the oral area," Zoe blew across the top of her hot chocolate. "Tough to say if you're doing it for him, if I'm being frank about it. I mean, how would you even know if he's excited? Or happy. Or sad. Mad. Any emotion really. Perhaps he injured his mouth by shaving his face after shaving his legs for a race or something."

Bea missed the sarcasm; she was too engrossed in her own thoughts. "I just don't know what the right thing to do is," she said, twirling her hair. "For Oliver, I mean. No Tong-, great, now I'm doing it. *Sam* is right. We spend most of our time together, but we waste a lot of it driving back and forth to each other's houses. It doesn't make much sense to have two places. I mean, what's not to like? He's nice. He's handsome. He's responsible. He's great with Oliver. He's got a decent job. He keeps himself in good shape. He's got a great place to live, much better than mine actually. He's willing to create a new movie room in it for Ollie and me. He's very accommodating."

"Accommodation. That's what I like in my men. That and baseline hygiene, and also near-average intelligence," Zoe leaned her head back slightly as she sprayed more whipped cream into the mug and then into her mouth.

"I know he's waiting for an answer. There're only so many evenings I can drink myself into oblivion or fake sleeping to buy time. He *deserves* an answer. I just don't want to do the wrong thing, you know? I hate the thought of choosing incorrectly," she paused. "Again." Bea frowned and looked visibly pained. "I can't keep putting it off. He's not going to wait forever."

Zoe grabbed Bea's hand from her hair and squeezed her fingers. "Aw, you'll figure it out, love. Or maybe he'll figure it out for you. Either way, I'm glad I ordered you that vibrating tongue toy for your birthday."

Snorting a laugh, Bea jerked her hand away from Zoe, snatching the whipped cream can.

Chapter 12

"Um, I'm sorry but I think my phone must be busted. You need my help with what?"

Lloyd paused, closed his eyes, and took a deep breath. He could feel Harold's wide smile through the connection and knew he would have a field day after he repeated the request. "I need you to help me pick up something I won on eBay."

"And what, again, did you say it was?" Harold's voice rose in anticipation.

Lloyd closed his eyes and paused. "A suit of armor."

Lloyd removed his phone from his ear as Harold's laughter peeled out of the speaker. He waited patiently while this continued until someone standing near Harold on his bluetooth must have worried he was psychotic and Lloyd heard him say, "What?!? I'm on the phone! Mind your own shit, man!" Harold paused briefly.

"And what, precisely, led you to purchase such a tremendously ridiculous object? Let me guess. Bea loves *Monty Python* and you're going to stand in her driveway 24/7 saying 'None shall pass!' until she agrees to get back together?" Harold had a laughing fit again. "What's next? Wait, wait...she loves *Elf* so you're gonna stop by Party City for a Santa suit then try to befriend a little person?"

Harold burst into laughter until he was forced into a coughing fit. When the coughing subsided and Harold had cleared his throat, Lloyd continued. "Nice Harold. Simultaneously awkward and prejudiced. Look, *how* I got the armor is a long story and not anything you'd really be interested in, so let's just work on the logistics."

"Oh, my friend. Try me," Harold chuckled.

"No time. I have no idea what this is gonna weigh, but I don't want to have to go to this guy's apartment twice in case it's a two person job. So, I need your help. Besides, my car is getting serviced anyway, so I need help with both weight and wheels."

Lloyd really hoped Harold wouldn't ask anything more about how he acquired the armor. His original interest was in purchasing an old military-issue motorbike with a sidecar so he could play out one of the early, classic *Garden State* scenes where Zach Braff and Natalie Portman start to build a rapport. He priced several, even bid on a couple on eBay, but when the auction end-time approached he panicked and pulled out. He knew there was no way he could ride a motorbike. Not in St. Louis, where traffic could be nuts even on the side streets. Not really anywhere, if he was honest about it. In fact, he was semi-paralyzed with anxiety just thinking about it. No, it had to be something else.

Weeks before, as he watched *Garden State* a second time, he made it past the motorcycle scene (where he turned it off the first time) and, lo and behold, saw one of his favorite actors, *The Big Bang Theory*'s Jim Parsons, enter the scene. Jim walks into the kitchen wearing a suit of armor after sleeping with another character's mother once his shift at the Renaissance-themed restaurant ended. Bingo. This hilarious scene he knew she loved was his in. He needed a suit of armor. The what-would-he-actually-do-with-a-suit-of-armor part he'd figure out soon enough, but he hadn't formed enough of a plan to believe he could convince Harold, so he simply pushed for the assistance.

"You shouldn't need any help. Let me break this down for you, Muchacho. A: People wear it. It is a *suit*, which means it was literally designed to be a one man job. Then again, that might explain why you can't do it alone," Harold jabbed. "Numero Dos: Don't give me this heavy lifting bullshit. You just want someone else to go with you because you're too much of a sissy to go anywhere alone. Again, a two person job in your case. I get it. I answered my own question. You need a man's help." Harold snorted and scratched himself. "Alright, fine. When is said pick-up?"

"Ideally, right now. I sent the guy an email saying I would be there before three."

"Sheesh. Okay, okay. Don't get your panties in a wad. I'll be there in 15 minutes. And, side note, since we're taking Miss Fisher and obviously your piece of shit is temporarily out of its misery – thank God - you're paying to have her hand washed on the way back. And if this results in the tiniest of scratches on her…"

"Oh, for God's sake, we're putting it *in* the car, not dangling it across the car." Lloyd interjected, feeling tired of Harold's constant focus on his red Plymouth Horizon convertible and the fact that he named her after Sacha

Baron Cohen's wife. "And please stop referring to your car as a person or I'll start referring to you 'Ginger Nuts'. I'll see you in fifteen."

The clink-clink sound preceded them by quite some distance as they made their way back toward Miss Fisher, interrupted only by Harold's stream of obscenities. "Tell me again, you son-of-a-bitch, why you didn't find it important to ask what floor this dude lived on when you set this up."

"Shut up and keep walking, Harold," Lloyd grunted. "Every time you stop to talk, you drip more sweat in between the welds and the thing's gonna start rusting 'cause God knows you're not gonna stop sweating. How romantic do you think it will be if I need you to follow me with a can of WD-40 as I walk toward her door?"

Harold laughed out loud. "Ha! So, you ARE gonna wear this thing? You are such a tool."

The sidewalk in front of the apartment complex measured no more than forty yards, but it took them a full fifteen minutes of huffing and puffing, pulling and sweating, to get from the previous owner's apartment door to Harold's Horizon.

"Now what, genius?" Harold said to Lloyd as they stood by the car and looked back and forth from the car to the armor. "Who was this armor originally made for, Andre the Giant? Don't tell me, that dude was the local president of *The Princess Bride* Fan Club."

"How would I know? You think I could understand a word he said? That guy was so stoned, he's still looking for the pizzas he thinks we delivered."

"Yeah, well at least he tipped us, which is what you're going to do when you get this fucking thing out of Miss Fisher," Harold said as he opened the door. "Now, hombre, let me be crystal clear here. You, my friend, are going to place this monstrosity into my passenger seat ever-so-delicately. Then you will be climbing into the backseat where you no-doubt will be pretzeled up to the point that you can smell your own ball sack."

"Well maybe if you didn't trade cars with women for sexual favors, you might have more room for passengers," Lloyd grunted, as he took the first stab at moving the suit's legs into the car.

"Shut up. Ass," Harold said with some bite, which let Lloyd know he'd better not mention it again.

Years ago, Harold lived briefly with a girl named Cheree, who was 18 inches shorter than him and pound-for-pound the same weight. Cheree owned this car and loved it for about two and a half weeks until, after numerous difficulties getting in and out of it, she convinced him that swapping her Horizon for his Rodeo was the only thing that was going to bring her happiness. Their relationship only lasted another three weeks or so, but long enough that she convinced Harold the deal was long-ago sealed. The loss of both his girl and his car was a bit much for Harold at the time, and it became apparent to Lloyd and others that Harold needed to love that car in order to maintain his sanity.

The two worked for a good twenty minutes manipulating the armor into the Horizon's front seat, taking turns yelling at one another until they finally wedged it into place. It consumed at least half of the front seat, with one knee pulled to its breastplate and a foot dangling parallel to the side mirror. Lloyd draped one of its arms around the driver's seat to anchor it, palm up. The other arm was wedged between the legs. After the third attempt finally allowed Lloyd to close the door, Harold glared at him. To avoid further conflict, Lloyd said nothing as he clambered over the trunk from the back of the convertible and wedged himself into the backseat.

Climbing into his driver's seat, Harold looked toward the armor and smiled for the first time since they arrived. "You know, it's actually not bad. Who knows? It might even be a chick magnet. Like a Renaissance wingman."

"Yeah, with you grinning like an idiot and his arm around you, you're the epitome of desirable, hetero-knighthood" Lloyd quipped. "Might as well slap a 'Dungeons and Dragons' bumper sticker on Miss Fisher's ass," Lloyd tried to yell over the wind and music, as Harold drove fast down Olive Boulevard, his car speakers blaring Europe's "The Final Countdown."

Since they couldn't exchange barbs effectively in the wind, Lloyd had plenty of time to delve into all the possibilities the acquisition of this suit represented. Perhaps he could show up outside her classroom wearing it and holding a bouquet of flowers, but he was uncertain if that had actually been done in any of her favorite films. He also wasn't exactly sure how he could get there wearing it. Lloyd was occasionally aware that Harold waved and nodded his head toward his new tin friend whenever a car passed with women inside, but he was busy brainstorming.

The possibility of wearing the suit with Oliver when she'd see it seemed most promising, but where? Maybe career day or open house at school? But he'd never get past the school metal detectors, and he was pretty sure the noise he would make at Oliver's next Jujitsu lesson would cause his expulsion from the dojo before she could even see him.

These thoughts engrossed him, so completely, in fact, that at first he had no idea why Harold yelled "Fuck!" and pulled the car over to the shoulder.

"What the fuck?!? Is there some law I don't know about that makes it illegal for three buds to drive down the highway waving at chicks?" Harold bitched as he put the car in park.

Lloyd touched his shoulder, "Harold, I'm worried about you. You do remember there is no one in the suit, right?"

"Of course, idiot," Harold said, but squinted at the armor and poked a finger through the eye hole. "You have to admit though, that thing was heavy enough to have had someone inside-" he stopped abruptly. "Oh no," he said, looking into his rear view mirror, his eyes sparkling. "Oh, this is too good. Too good," a huge smile spread rapidly across his face, making Lloyd incredibly curious, and a little worried.

As he turned around in his seat that worry turned quickly into massive anxiety, then utter devastation, as he saw the police officer pulling them over. He was not just any police officer. Oh, no. That would be too clean. It had to be Sam Dunbar dismounting his BMW-R900.

Harold practically smacked his lips in anticipation of the interaction.

"Why hello, officer...Dunbar, is it? What seems to be the problem, your eminence?" Harold laid on the charm while Lloyd rested his head in his hand and tried to seem nonchalant. He did everything possible to disappear into the backseat, which was difficult to do with his head between his legs.

"License and registration, please. Did you know you have a taillight out, sir?" Sam said, his voice edged with curiosity as he peered past Harold to stare at the armor.

"No, I had no idea! Did *you* know that light was out, Lloyd Stanley?" Harold said, as he handed his paperwork to Sam and pivoted in his seat.

Sam glanced quickly at the license and then looked directly at Lloyd. "Lloyd Stanley? Ex-husband of Bea Stanley? I think we might have met once." Sam momentarily forgot the interaction and extended his hand to Lloyd, who shook it awkwardly. "I'm Sam, Bea's...uh, boyfriend."

"Great, hey, yeah, nice to meet you," Lloyd said quickly, his lips pursed into a semi-smile.

"So, what's with the knight? I have to be honest. When I first saw the hand draped around your shoulder, I thought someone was sitting there flipping me off," Sam chuckled.

"Oh, Lloyd here thought it would be great if-," Harold was cut off by the sudden appearance of Lloyd's knee to the back of his driver's seat. "Ow! I think he's in a hurry. You see, he's a new member of that Dagorhir medieval reenactment group that meets in Forest Park

Saturday mornings. Did Bea tell you? Oh, perhaps she forgot to mention that about her ex. He's *totally* into that now. You know what, she might not know, so feel free to tell her. Anyway, every time the wizard beats him into submission during their role play at the park, they make him wear just the helmet throughout the next reenactment, so he's pretty antsy to get there. He just kept pushing me to go faster. Sorry if I was over the speed limit by a hair when you saw us."

"Ohh-kay. Well, I'll just give you a warning today, but be sure to get that light fixed, alright?" Sam ripped the warning off the pad and handed it to Harold, then looked at Lloyd. "So, have fun, and I'll tell Bea you said hello. Have a nice day, guys."

"Absolutely. You too, Officer Dunbar," Harold said, ripping the warning into pieces as Sam walked back to his motorcycle. He turned to Lloyd. "You know, I take back what I said earlier. I'll pay for Miss Fisher's hand washing today, because that was *so* worth every single excruciating second." He cracked up as he started the motor again.

"Yeah, well, you can keep the armor, too, and just drop me off at the library," Lloyd said, dejectedly. He closed his eyes and hit his head repeatedly against the back of Harold's headrest as they drove away.

Lloyd tried to appear nonchalant as he strolled with the librarian, Veronica, through the back of the library through the archived LPs and DVDs. They were close enough for their sleeves to touch, but he seemed oblivious. He was on a mission.

"Let's see if I can assist," Veronica said, scanning the shelf. "*Titanic?*"

"Too widespread in its celebration," Lloyd said.

"*The Notebook?*"

"Don't think so. Same. Plus she thought it was too predictable."

"Oh, and *Titanic* wasn't?" Veronica grinned, but Lloyd was too befuddled to appreciate the humor. She paused, processing, tilted her head, and turned toward him, "So, she likes romantic movies, but she doesn't like them if they're too mainstream."

"Something like that," Lloyd felt a bit uncomfortable talking about Bea to Veronica, but he thought, being a librarian, perhaps she could guide him to greater success than he was experiencing on his own. "She sometimes says, 'if it ends the way most people think it should, it isn't a good ending'. Whatever that means."

Veronica ran her fingertips across a few movie cases as her mind worked to decode the riddle he was experiencing. She sighed lightly. "Yes, I guess I can understand her perspective. Well, then, let's see," they continued to walk, slowly and methodically, perusing the shelves. "Hey! You could totally go old school. Tracy and Hepburn, that sort of thing. Mainstream at the time, of course, but not in our era."

"Maybe. Although, probably not. Hepburn's kind of sacred ground, actually," Lloyd said as his mind turned to all those times Bea had asked him to watch *The Philadelphia Story* with her, and all the times he pushed for something else. Hell, Bea even had a framed poster of *Roman Holiday* in her home office. He put his hand to his forehead as he scanned the shelf. "Ooh, *Harold & Maude!* Now *this* is what I'm talking about. Well, not this specifically. That won't work. But, do you have something like this? This is her thing."

"60 year age gaps between love interests is her thing?" Veronica cocked an eyebrow and smirked.

"No, no. I mean she's totally into this film, Smarty-Pants."

Veronica feigned irritation, "You know, I don't think you know me well enough to call me Smarty-Pants, Mr. Stan Lee. For all you know, I could be a Dummy-Pants."

"Sorry," Lloyd said, and his face dropped a bit.

"Just teasing," she said, briefly touching his shoulder. "Lighten up a little. I actually own my smarty-pants-ness."

"What I meant is she uses it in her classes and stuff. Like *every* semester," Lloyd smiled and felt re-energized.

"What does she teach?" Veronica asked.

"Communication," Lloyd said beaming

"What kind of communication? Like Media Criticism?"

"What? Oh, uh, sure. Maybe. Speech and gender and stuff like that," Lloyd's eyed the DVD case hungrily.

Veronica looked puzzled, "She uses *Harold & Maude* in a speech class? That seems a little strange. What does she use it for?"

Lloyd shifted his weight uncomfortably. "Uh, I don't know. I just know she always had it, I mean, has it in her bag," he confessed with a blush. He put the DVD back on the shelf. He suddenly felt guilty, although he couldn't pinpoint why.

"Remind me again what you're trying to accomplish?" Veronica turned her body toward him and gave him her full attention. "I don't quite understand. You're trying to find her favorite movies so you can watch them with her?"

"It's, well-," as before in his interaction with Veronica, Lloyd couldn't find a way to describe his project that wouldn't sound weird or pathetic. "As I said, it's complicated. How about this? What are some rom-coms you like? Maybe that will help."

Veronica looked at him again, raised her eyebrows and shook her head slightly as she turned toward the shelf. "Well," she paused, sighed, and scanned the shelf, "I'm probably not the right person to ask. Maybe you should ask her." She continued staring his direction, but he seemed oblivious. She took a few more steps. "To be fair, if I'm going rom-com, I'm probably going Johnny Depp. *Chocolat? Benny & Joon?*"

"*Benny & Joon!*" Lloyd grabbed it from her hand. "That one I *know* she loves. Sold," Lloyd exclaimed and headed toward the checkout desk.

Veronica followed him, still looking a little confused. She scanned the movie into the checkout system and handed it to him, but held onto it a few seconds longer when he grabbed it. "Good luck, Stan Lee." She gave him a small wave as he walked out the door, then sighed to herself. "Sounds like you're going to need it."

Chapter 13

Bea had been staring blankly out the window for several minutes. Outside, her eyes took in all the pruning she never got around to during the summer and fall. She had a beautiful back yard area with tons of space for flowers and trees and a swing hanging on an A-frame. She bought it specifically to give Oliver room to explore, but it was a heck of a lot of work. When she first bought the place, just after the divorce finalized, she felt more energized knowing the work she was putting in was for her and for Oliver, knowing that she made all the decisions, and that she was a strong, independent woman who could do anything. About a year after that, it basically just made her stomach turn, knowing all the work that awaited her when the ground thawed.

But now, as she stood in her bedroom packing storage containers, she felt an odd mixture of emotions. Relief, since she wouldn't have to get the yard back into shape come spring. She wouldn't have to get any yard into shape, come to think of it, because Sam absolutely loved gardening and his yard was already immaculate. Then, irritation, because she actually hated yardwork and always had to take care of it all, even when she was still married to Lloyd. He was always complaining of his allergies, of snakes in the back ditch that could come up and sink their fangs into him, of the heat, of wasps. That was quickly followed by satisfaction, which she attributed to the fact that she chose to leave Lloyd. Before remorse could fully declare its presence, she heard Sam whistling his way down her hallway and she began packing the storage boxes again.

"Hey, babe. Are you sure you want to wait for a moving truck? That's, like, at least six weeks away. Seriously, I could move a car load of stuff every few days, starting with all this Christmas stuff. It'll save you, us, a lot of money."

Bea smiled over her shoulder while she folded the stockings and placed them lovingly into the box. "Oh, no thanks. It costs the same for the truck no matter how full it is. Might as well make them earn their money, right?" That should be enough of an explanation that he won't ask any more about the hesitation, she thought. "Besides, I still need these last few weeks to sort through stuff, see what I can give away to Zoe or Goodwill, maybe create a garage sale pile. And, I still have to get Lloyd to sign off on the address change. Lots of little things to do."

She grinned, but inside she worried way more about Lloyd than the money. She and Lloyd had always filed their own paperwork, always shared a lawyer and agreed on most everything, at least after a bit of back and forth. Part of that was a result of her commitment to maintaining close ties. She ensured Lloyd could ask for Oliver anytime he wanted and not have him when he didn't. She invited him over to have dinner with them on occasion. She gave him his own house key, in case they ever needed anything while she was traveling to conferences or simply wanted to use the movie room. She did it to ensure minimal disruption to their relationship. Or, perhaps, to ensure minimal disruption to the co-parent relationship. Minimal disruption to her interpersonal relationship with Lloyd? She didn't spend much time dwelling on what lay at the core of it.

All she knew was, without a doubt, she dreaded having this particular conversation with Lloyd. This felt almost bigger than the divorce itself. Certainly it was bigger than convincing him they needed to sell the brick, two-story house they used to share. Lloyd had worked hard to sell Bea on the idea that a move like that could be a great opportunity for a new start together, a clean slate. She shut that down, of course. Redirected the conversation anytime Lloyd suggested they use a life change like that as a time to try again.

This, though…this was different. This was a new structure. Lloyd might have mistaken their lines as intersecting before when Bea thought they were parallel, but this was a triangle, and far more stressful to mention. Which is why, in all honesty, she had yet to do it; why she had been very careful to talk with Oliver about it somewhat vaguely: getting a newer house, a nicer room, how cool would that be? Bea knew Oliver always shared bits and pieces of their conversations with Lloyd, and they often came out so twisted and convoluted that Lloyd didn't bother to ask for what truth lay within. Also, for the last couple of months, she had worked diligently to avoid putting herself in a situation where they had time to discuss anything in length. She put it off at pickups and drop-offs, saying she had to get to grading, making a quick call on her cell right when pulling up in his apartment parking lot so she was on the phone and "unavailable," but, time was running out, and she knew there would be no easy way to put it off much longer.

Sam slipped his arms around her waist from behind, kissed her shoulder, and they both looked out at the yard. Bea sighed. "I'm gonna miss seeing that purple clematis covering the trellis this summer."

"I'll bet. It's a beautiful plant; even *you* can grow it," Sam joked and nibbled on her shoulder as she nudged her elbow into his ribs. "Seriously, though, I was thinking we could take a few clippings of it and…"

Sam continued explaining how he would do the clippings and where he'd plant the starts, and Bea occasionally said "mm-hm," but she didn't really hear him. She was busy remembering how proud she had felt buying this house on her own. A clean break from her past. Oliver loved the swing, the movie room. She had allowed him to choose the paint for his bedroom and had even painted a picture frame on a low part of the wall in the hallway, and every few months or so she let him paint a new picture inside it directly onto the wall. To encourage Oliver's creativity, she had even decided to do her own temporary painting on the ceiling in that hallway, and they had a fantastic time painting and singing together on several occasions. She incorporated viewing and praising Oliver's masterpiece into every house tour and repeatedly poked fun at her own artistic inadequacies when guests visited. Her brow crinkled slightly as she wondered about Sam's reaction if she tried to do that in his hallway. His immaculate hallway. She hoped it wouldn't take too long for Oliver and her to feel like it was their hallway and for Sam to be okay with it no longer being immaculate. A newer, bigger house. A newer, bigger life on a quiet cul-de-sac.

"…so that will look awesome by the fish pond. Anyway, what time is it, babe? I've gotta run home and grab a few things. Aren't you supposed to pick up Oliver around four-thirty?" Sam asked.

"Yes! God, I must be tired. I'm feeling a little spacey. Just leave the rest of the decorations. I'll take them down tomorrow. Be back in a few, 'kay?" Bea kissed his cheek as she walked out of the room, and she could hear him whistling some pop country song as she closed her front door.

Lloyd opened his apartment door right as Bea's hand went up to knock. "Oh, hey! Wow! That was great timing, huh?" Lloyd tried to beam at her but winced a little when he smiled.

"What in the world happened to your lip? C'mon, Little Man!" Bea yelled past Lloyd for Oliver but couldn't stop staring at Lloyd, whose bottom lip looked like a pink cucullia caterpillar. "Did you and Harold get into a fight at Bath & Body Works again?"

Lloyd paused for a split second, overcome by a flashback of the angry grandmother who whizzed the lotion bottle and scented candle at Harold's head. "No, no. I just slipped. In the shower. You know, wet floor, not so graceful. Bad combination."

Lloyd quickly turned to zip Oliver's jacket to avoid making direct eye contact with Bea. She could always tell when he was lying. There was no way he was going to tell her the truth. As it was, after watching *Benny & Joon* a few times he attempted his first suave, Keaton-esque chair walkover so he could perform it for her the next time she stopped by. However, he fell face-first onto the coffee table, and busted his lip wide open.

"Anyway, we were just thinking of heading to Chick-Fil-A. Want to come with us? Oliver can play while you tell me all about your spring classes, who's driving you crazy already, who has given you the best excuse for missing class…c'mon, it'll be great."

"No, thanks. If it's okay with you, we need to get going. Tonight is Asscar at Zoe's." Despite the many worries weighing on her mind, Bea couldn't stop herself from smiling just thinking about Zoe's party and how much she looked forward to it each year. "Ollie-Boll, go get your Leap Pad, okay?" Bea watched Oliver run into his room. Knowing he had a room at his dad's that was separate than his room at home always made her feel blind, disconnected, like a clique-less teenager searching for a seat in the cafeteria. She looked at her boots and shuffled her feet hesitantly. "So, I wanted to let you know I'm putting my house on the market. I haven't said anything yet to Oliver because I don't know how long it will take to sell, but I thought you should know since he'll probably mention it to you as soon as the sign goes up in the yard."

Lloyd felt a sudden panic. He wanted to know everything and nothing. He stopped himself from asking about things he didn't want to hear. Instead he tried to sound nonchalant. "Oh, you're moving?"

"Yeah, I don't know the details yet. It's just time for a change."

"You're staying in the area, though. Just getting a bigger place or something?"

Bea watched Oliver walking toward them, "Yeah, I'm just looking into options. We- we can grab a coffee and talk about it soon." She couldn't get off the porch fast enough. "Okay, give your dad a hug and come jump in the car. See ya, Lloyd." Bea tried to sound incredibly friendly. She was worried if she didn't Lloyd might get too panicky and want to hear everything right now.

Lloyd opened his mouth but no words came out. His mind raced as he watched her car pull out. Bea's car had distinctive headlights. She had purchased that used Acura when she was pregnant with Oliver, getting rid of the ancient Ford Escort, which required pulling onto the shoulder every ten miles or so during the coldest months to spray lubricant into the throttle body.

The Acura's previous owner had retrofitted it with high-intensity discharge, green-tinged headlights. They glowed like Chevy Chase's toxic eyes in *Modern Problems.* Lloyd wanted her to leave the headlights as-is, as research he did seemed to indicate they were safer. Bea didn't put much stock into the research, but she was fond of the green glow and said she felt like she was driving some sort of super car. That was fortunate for Lloyd, as they always stood out in a line of cars. He could always tell when it was her coming toward him.

Tonight they were the brightest of greens. Green like envy personified. The glow of her headlights leaving shone into his chest, and he momentarily wondered if they had the capability of filling him with some sort of supernatural envy energy that would propel him through the air to crash-land in the middle of the street like the Hulk, stopping her from leaving.

Moving? Where? Why? With whom? It's got to be with that douchebag cop, that "Sam" character. Damn it. This is it.

His brain felt like scrambled eggs as he tried to come up with just the right thing to do. And fast. He mentally scrolled through movies he had previously discarded as he watched her taillights moving away from him.

But just before she was out of sight, a monstrous flock of birds, squawking loudly in song, took flight across the pink winter sunset just behind her car. It was massive and magical. He knew, had she seen it, she would have loved it. He snatched his phone out of his pocket and tried to record it, but he wasn't fast enough. So he decided to call her and describe it. After four rings he knew she wasn't going to answer, and as her voicemail picked up the speed of his speech was fueled by the fantastic visual event and his panic.

"Bea! Oh, you should have picked up; you might have been able to see it! You just missed it! Right when you left this wall of birds flew up behind your car. It was incredible! There had to be at least 10,000 birds, and they were haloed in this pink glow from the sunset. Amazing!" He paused, unsure what to say next. "You, you should have seen it. Okay. Well, have a nice time at Zoe's. Bye."

He hung up and felt worse. Asscar Fest was the one time of the year he bonded with Zoe, their mutual proficiency in all movie trivia trumping her typical disinterest and mild disdain. *But tonight, he'll be there. At Zoe's. Next to Bea. In my place.* He closed the door and fell onto the couch with a groan.

Asscar Fest was Zoe's annual anti-Oscar soiree. Each year the weekend before the Annual Academy Awards aired, Zoe invited all her friends to come over dressed down, walk her pink fuzzy carpet, eat junk food, drink cheap booze, and watch the year's worst movies. After going home to change clothes and grab his hand-me-down Gloworm, Bea and Oliver headed west to pick up Sam for the evening's events.

Sam walked toward Bea's car, then stopped and bowed in his blue pin-striped pajamas. She smiled in approval at his clothing choice. He climbed in, carrying a case of Keystone and a gift bag, closed the door, and kissed Bea's cheek.

"Nice hoodie, babe. Is that a pizza stain?"

"Blue paint. My old favorite painting clothes. The stain matches my Gonzo slippers perfectly, don't you think?" Bea smiled in the dark as they headed toward Zoe's.

Sam looked down at her feet. "Muppets. Classic, but are they safe to drive in? In fact," he feigned seriousness and turned a bit so Oliver could hear him, "I think that's against the law to drive without real shoes on, ma'am. What do you think, Oliver? Should I give your Mom a ticket?"

"Driving without shoes is not against the laws, but if she has a accident she could have a citation." Oliver cited from memory, distracted and playing his Leap Pad.

Sam did a double-take then pivoted around and stared at Bea.

Bea shook her head. "Yeah, I know; strange, huh? But there is an explanation. Lloyd's friend Harold gave Sam a *Rules of the Road* book for his fifth birthday. I think he hoped Ollie would annoy Lloyd by calling out any rule he was breaking while driving. Of course, now that you've met Harold, that probably doesn't surprise you. So what's in the bag? Mad Dog 20/20? No, wait, Everclear?"

"Actually, it's a surprise for Zoe."

"Really?" Bea said with a smirk.

"Well, you know she hasn't really warmed up to me yet."

Bea made a quick attempt to frown and dispute Sam's comment, but he stopped her. "Don't worry, it's obvious. I just saw something I thought she'd like, that's all. Can't blame a guy for trying."

"Look at you, trying to impress my friends!" Bea shoved his shoulder teasingly and Sam shook it off with a smile.

"Besides, don't worry, babe. I brought you a present, too. Jealous girl," he winked at her and pulled a CD out of the gift bag. "Ta da!"

Bea laughed when she saw the PINK CD, not because he brought her something, but because it was an album by PINK. At first she felt a strong wave of connectedness to Sam because for the first time she was convinced he not only understood the purpose of Asscar night, but he was embracing it fully. She kept smiling at him as he excitedly ripped the cellophane off the case.

"I know you don't have it because I took a sneak peek at your phone and your CD shelf and it wasn't there. 'It's All Your Fault' is one of my favorites," Sam popped the CD in the car and whistled to it as they drove toward Zoe's.

That's when Bea realized he seriously liked it. Like, *seriously* liked it. Bea tried to show her appreciation by tapping her fingers on the steering wheel in time to the music. She couldn't bring herself to point out that PINK really wasn't her cup of tea, and she was confident several of the songs on the disc were ones she had previously included among the worst things she'd heard on the radio last year. Bea could have found irony and humor in this inadvertent Asscar-like celebration of crap music, but instead it made her slightly nauseous.

Oliver was the first to Zoe's door and rang her doorbell five times in beat to "Shave and a Haircut," to which Zoe always knocked back the last two beats from her side of the door. "Lollie-lol! Awesome Superman costume! You will definitely win the Most Creatively Dressed on the Pink Carpet Award tonight, my friend. Entrer, entrer! Dr. Jones's little girl, Emma, and your buddy Tyler are already in the basement playing foosball, and I have Scooby Doo queued up on Netflix. Just press the button that looks like a house on the remote, okay?" Zoe tousled his hair as he walked past in his cape. "I'll bring you all some Pringles and Fitz's root beer in just a tic, lovey," she yelled over her shoulder as she hugged Bea, who snorted a laugh as she took in Zoe's ensemble: polka dotted MC Hammer pants and a white sleeveless undershirt. "My sweet BB. Those plaid sweatpants are to die for. You brought your jammies, correct?"

"Absolutely."

"And Samuel, excellent beverage selection. Well played, sir, along with those superb, manly pajamas, and, I see you come bearing gifts!"

Sam handed her the gift bag, and when Zoe opened it her face visibly softened. "Oh, my! This is fabulous! My very own Asscar! Look, everyone, my very own Asscar!"

Out of the bag she pulled a delicate crystal female figurine whose stance was reminiscent of that of an Oscar. She turned toward her living room and said in a voice loud enough to be heard by the two couples near the TV and the trio in her kitchen, "Gosh! Where do I begin? I'd like to thank God, of course, because I'll never have to be on that movie set again, and my perv-y Uncle Wilfred. There's no way I could have made it through those difficult scenes without his teachings." Her guests all laughed and went back to their chatter. Zoe turned to Sam, "Where on earth did you get this, Samuel? Did you commission someone to sculpt me in class when I wasn't looking, you cheeky monkey?" she winked at him and raised her eyebrows at Bea.

Sam laughed abashedly. "No, nothing like that. I just saw it today and thought you would like it for your party."

"Well, it's lovely, thank you, Sam. Please, my friends, make yourselves settled. Munch, mingle, imbibe," Zoe said, as she walked in front of them into the living room where most of the other guests gathered.

Bea looked at Sam befuddled while she found a place to put her coat. "Where in the world could you have been today that had crystal figurines? Was it the same place where you got all the crystal for your house? I've heard of crystal junkies, but I always thought that meant something different."

"Yeah, I have a connection." Sam quickly shifted topics and darted after Zoe, "So what's on the watch list tonight? I have to admit, I'm not up on all the movies, and I try to choose the ones I do pay for carefully."

"Oh, we've got some doozies tonight, my friend," she turned to proclaim to her guests. "Attention, all. Tonight's feature presentations will begin for your viewing pleasure in approximately thirty minutes. First up is this year's Worst Picture Winner: *Grown Ups.*" Groans and chuckles filled the room, but, while Zoe meandered around showing off her figurine to the party-goers, Sam grabbed Bea's arm.

"Hey," he whispered. "I thought the point was to watch the crappiest movies of last year at this party."

Bea cocked her head, "It is. Why?"

"What?!? No way. *Grown Ups?!?* That was my favorite movie last year," Sam said, looking confused.

Bea raised her eyebrows and shrugged her shoulders. "Well, I guess, uh, to each his own." She grabbed one of his Keystones and headed toward the living room.

"Book worms," Sam said to the beer in the empty room. "At least I'll get to spend my evening watching great movies."

Chapter 14

"Hey, doofus!" Lloyd's mouse went flying out of his hand and under his desk as Harold, as always, slammed his arm down on the top of Lloyd's cubicle wall.

"Harold, for fu-," Lloyd began, then took a deep breath and climbed under his desk to get his mouse. Grabbing the side of his keyboard tray as he emerged, he spit his words through gritted teeth. "How many times do I need to say it? Stop doing that. Just say, 'Hey.' I promise I'll turn around." He sat down again and turned back to his computer.

"Whatever. Hey, riddle me this, Sherlock. What's black and white and *read* all over?"

Lloyd sighed, "I don't have time for this, Harold. I have work to do."

Harold leaned in, "Aw, c'mon, you *know* you want to know. What's black and white and *read* all over? C'mon," Harold taunted.

"I have no earthly idea."

"The side of a Two Men and a Truck moving van driving around town. You know, the kind that your ex-wife just hired for a partial pack. Get it? Get it?" Harold grinned and slapped him hard on the back. "$500 just for the deposit. Kinda pricey, don't you think? My question is, wouldn't you think they'd have enough testosterone-riddled buddies around that they could move shit for free? And, how much are cops around here getting paid?" Harold paused and stared off momentarily. "Maybe I should consider a well-timed career change."

Lloyd turned to glare at him as he glanced nervously toward the surrounding cubicles. "Harold! I told you to stop looking at her debit card purchases! You're going to get us both fired, you asshole."

"Relax, compadre! Do you really think Big Brother monitors all the shit we look at 40 hours a week? Jesus! How fucking boring would that job be? Paying someone to watch people watch people watch other people's transactions, genius? Why would they pay two people to look at the *same* shit? Chillax. This company is *way* too cheap for that. Besides, truth be told, I think you're just cranky because Queen B is 'moving' on without you," he faked weeping, dabbing his eyes. "Either that, or it's your time of the month," he said as he shoved his hand into Lloyd's M&M bowl and put a fistful into his mouth.

"Just cool it with the private investigation, okay?" Lloyd shook his head and turned back around.

"I keep telling you, man," Harold said through a mouthful of chocolate, "everything you need to know is there. See what she's doing, guess what she'll do next, and bingo. You are where you need to be, doing what you need to be doing. Predictive analysis. Say it with me, pre-dic-tive a-nal-y-sis. Target does it. Google does it. And you can do it, too."

"That's stupid. Likely, in this case, illegal. And at the very least, unethical," Lloyd said, keeping his back to Harold.

"Suit yourself," Harold said as he walked away, "but if you want her at any cost, going big data is a hell of a lot smarter than pretending to be DiCaprio, Romeo."

Lloyd sighed heavily as Harold walked away, then paused as he thought of Target's response to the implementation of their own formula when they got called out in the media over marketing to that pregnant teenager. Their marketing guru said predictive analytics was proven to work….as long as the shopper didn't get spooked first. He paused momentarily, thinking through the rewards versus the spooking. *No way,* he thought as he stared at his in-box. *I've got another chance with this movie scene concept. This time, I'll recreate just the right moment, the stars will be aligned, and Bea will find her way back to me. With a move eminent, this has to work.*

It took him a while to realize he'd been looking at the same line of data ad infinitum without moving a muscle, so he decided to grab a cup of coffee, push those thoughts back, and start working again. If he didn't, he realized, this cup of coffee might soon turn into a job at Starbucks.

Back at home that evening, Lloyd dug into his hardcopy movie quote book, hoping it would fan the flames of his passion-driven creativity. Into the wee hours of the morning he flipped pages, scribbled on post-it notes, and plowed through two bowls of chips and salsa seeking his plan's salvation and a movie that would speak to Bea.

"What? Why this? This isn't right," Lloyd complained as he climbed up into the black and tan 1920s Peugeot and plopped down next to Harold.

"What are you blathering on about, Bro?" Harold said. "We have a driver, we're in Paris, it's a beautiful night, and we're in a pimped out ride. *With*, might I add, an apparently unlimited supply of whiskey and Cuban cigars. The only thing I see wrong with this is that *you* are the one climbing in and not a hot Parisian babe wearing nothing but a fur coat." Ice clinked in Harold's glass as he tipped back his drink. "Plus, we're not drinking absinthe or wearing elaborate makeup or singing and dancing, so at least we know this isn't a Baz Lurhmann film. Which is nice. It could be a hell of a lot worse." He poured another glass.

"No, no. I know this isn't *Moulin Rouge*. We're obviously smack dab in the middle of *Midnight in Paris*. Look at us, how we're dressed, where we are. Look at the mist outside and the soft glow of the lamp lights. We're practically made of watercolors. Woody might as well be in the front of the Peugeot telling us how to sit and what to say. But I don't get it. I already crossed this one off my list, so I have no idea why I'm even thinking about it. I know I'm desperate for a movie scene I can riff off of, but this is too risky. Owen Wilson loses his original girl in the end," he said, confused and whining. "No, this won't work at all. I'm running out of time," Lloyd looked out the window. "God, I'll bet I'm lying there on my couch right now in my apartment, drooling on that stupid movie quote book. I've got to get my shit together, because osmosis isn't getting me anywhere. I don't have time for this. I'm dying here," Lloyd said and rubbed his face with his hands.

"Dude! Stop being such a wuss. It's unmanly!" Harold's voice dropped. "Show some courage and grace under pressure, for God's sake! If she is meant for you, declare her meant for you! If your love is true and real, it will create a respite from death," he took a swig of his whiskey, smacked his lips, and smirked, "or some shit like that. Damn! I make a good Hemingway. At least you held it together enough through this crazy, hallucinated movie-dream not to make me what's-her-face...who did Cathy Bates play again?" He cracked his neck and straightened his collar as the car bounced along the cobbled streets. "All I can say is, you obviously fell asleep because you're exhausted by your own idiocy."

Lloyd stared dejectedly out the window at the streets of Paris.

"So now what, genius?" Harold said.

"Now I need to figure out why I'm here, and it's not for the whiskey or the Peugeot," Lloyd said toward the window. "Aw, the hell with it. As far as I know, I just fell asleep on the Woody Allen page of my movie quote book. Simple as that. This obviously means nothing."

They rolled along quietly for a few minutes before Lloyd jerked forward and spoke again. "Wait. We're in Paris, right?"

"Duh," Harold said before he burped into his fist and lit a cigar.

"And we're writers. In the *Midnight in Paris* movie, I mean."

"This is apparently true, my friend. You are a modern-day teller of stories, and I your confidante, fresh from war with a heart overflowing with character and testosterone."

Lloyd looked at him and then back out the window as they passed the Shakespeare and Company bookstore. "Oh, man. Bingo! That's brilliant! Wow, my subconscious must be working overtime! I rock, if I do say so myself."

"Care to elaborate on the sudden boost of confidence, or should I even ask?" Harold puffed his cigar.

"This isn't about *Midnight in Paris*. It's about *Before Sunset,* another of Bea's favorites. You've seen it, right? Set in Paris. It was one of the movies Bea and I could always agree to watch. The whole story begins as the main character describes to an audience inside that bookstore right there, Shakespeare and Company, what it was like to lose his true love. I looked it up two or three years ago when Bea was planning a trip to France to give some sort of talk. Shakespeare and Company. It's 100 years old and all the same famous writers in Woody Allen's movie actually used to hang out there. James Joyce, Hemingway, the whole crew. How freakin' awesome is that?"

"Wait, did you just say the dude in *Before Sunset* lost his chick? I thought that wasn't allowed by your ridiculous rules."

"Ah, yes. But in *Before Sunset* it's completely obvious to everyone that the romantic leads are destined to be together. I mean, these characters just can't stand to be apart. Granted, the outcome is a little vague, but the chemistry is undeniable. It's right up Bea's alley. Perfect," Lloyd said, and his whole body relaxed.

"So now what? You're gonna fly her to Paris and drive her around bookstores in a Peugeot? That's moronic, even for you," Harold shook his head and worked to make smoke circles.

"All I know is I need to wake myself up. Then I'll watch *Before Sunset* again and figure the rest out. I need to go grab a copy, though. I lost mine in the 'war.'"

"That's too obscure, even for a douche-y movie geek like you. You're reaching, bro," Harold snorted and shook his head.

"I told you my strength as the Lord of Worthless Movie Minutiae would save me someday. This may be surreal, but it's going to be fantastic."

"Lloyd, old man," Harold gave Lloyd's knee a couple of heavy pats and took deep puffs on his cigar, "did it ever occur to you that perhaps your leading character in *Before Sunset* wrote the book and shared it in the bookstore because he was destined to tell stories about loss and love and living well, and that perhaps that is what your own beloved admires most?"

"Whoa. You've really got this Hemingway thing down. You're starting to creep me out a little bit. You're also off base. Pay attention, Harold. Hello! Bea calls herself a helpless romantic during her first conversations with everyone she meets, right? She's in it for the love, man. Without a doubt."

Harold shrugged, "Fair enough. I wish you the best of fortunes, my friend," Harold stretched forward and tapped the driver's shoulder. "You can drop me off here, at the Rotonde." As the car came to a stop, he climbed out groaning. "I need a nightcap after putting up with all your horse shit or I just might shoot myself."

"Zoe, ready for lunch?" Bea asked from Zoe's office doorway, then stopped and leaned toward Zoe's computer screen. "Uh, what, pray tell, are you up to?' she asked, with a quizzical smile.

"I'll tell you what it is, lovey. It's my salvation. Frankly, the men on this campus are so bloody stupid that I can't be bothered trying to spend any more time with them. In fact, I am absolutely convinced at this point in my life that PhD in men actually stands for Phallic Dysfunction."

Bea chuckled. "So what are you going to do about it?"

"What I am going to do about it is to make all of this miraculousness," displaying her body with her hands, "available to the worthy souls populating the interweb." Zoe brought her hands to her computer screen. "Why waste all this when I could offer it up to men who actually have social skills, a real paycheck, and working genitalia? Look. I'm just about to hit submit. Check it."

Bea looked over the dating write-up Zoe had written for this particular site. "Let's see. *Sexual maven with nomadic tendencies' ...*I'm afraid to spend any time at all thinking through what that means," Bea said, "'*seeking a propitious playmate for confabulating and whistle-wetting. Self-proclaimed prodigies and Gods' gifts to women need not apply. Savvy students of Thom Yorke and the Donut Stop's 'Cinnamon Glob' will be moved to the front of the class.* "She raised her eyebrows and shrugged at Zoe. "It's unique, I'll grant you that. Aren't you afraid students will read this?"

"What, our students? Doubtful, since it's not selfie-friendly. Besides, even if they did, they would move on because they wouldn't know what half of those words mean." They both smiled.

Bea clicked on the logo. "What is this site, anyway? It's called, let's see, O³. Wait, didn't I hear that was short for OutOfOptions or OverOurOptimism or something?"

"As if! O³, darling, is hip for OnOurOwn.com. Or is it OpenOurOptions? Who knows, who cares? I'll tell you what it's not, and that's staring at the same stupid faces eating their General Tso's chicken in the cafeteria every arvo, that's what. I just need to add my pic-y, and...done. Now we sit back and watch the hot commodities roll in," Zoe smiled and put her feet up on her desk.

"I thought you said it didn't include selfies," Bea leaned in. "Zoe, you didn't post your own picture. That's a picture of Sailor Moon in a schoolgirl uniform."

"Yeah! What did you think? That I was going to upload my performance pic from last year's Western Conference? As if! Nah, see, that is what I love about this site. You cruise through looking for people with similar interest in important things like sexual position preference, or how quickly you buy your Bonnaroo tickets, or how vehemently you believe *Heroes* jumped the shark faster than any other show in NBC history. Let's get real. We all know if you put a picture there you'll just go by appearance alone, then you'll end up selecting someone who looks like Channing Tatum and acts like Charlie Sheen. So why not just assume you may hook up with someone from whom you'll cringe a bit in the cold light of morning and instead focus on criterion that is truly important. Like tolerable body odor if trapped in an elevator for over thirty minutes."

"Then, you'd better avoid the cafeteria's garlic shrimp at lunch. Your perfect match might send you an after-class drink invitation by the time we get back," Bea chuckled, buttoning her coat.

Zoe hit enter with a flourish and grabbed her purse. "Don't be jealous, dear. Who knows what bliss a search for *'fans of a little tongue now and again'* could ultimately bring to your own life?" she said as Bea shoved her playfully down the hall.

"Dr. Stanley, a word please."

Bea walked toward the Liberal Arts office smiling broadly. She heard the dean ask for her while she was standing outside and exited Zoe's office. They had just returned from a nice lunch and walk, during which Zoe regaled Bea with details from last weekend's Buffalo Wild Wing's faculty trivia showdown. Upon their return, Zoe had checked her O^3 inbox and discovered five immediate "winks," one *'we should hang'* virtual sign board, and one note inviting her to meet up at the

Wolf Public Coffee House on Saturday. As she read them off to Bea she broke into a vigorous Bollywood fusion dance contained within the five-by-two foot area between her wall and her desk. Bea watched, giggling in amazement, and her smile lingered with her down the hall and into Dean Powell's office.

"Hey, Dean Powell. Happy Wednesday. How goes it today?"

"Well, that all remains to be seen, my dear Dr. Stanley."

"Oh, no," Bea froze. "Don't tell me I've had more students up here fighting during lunch."

"No, no. Nothing like that," Dean Powell said, squinting at her. He straightened a skull and bronze-plated trowel at the corner of his desk and inhaled deeply. "No, my day depends in part on your verification or denial of some interesting rumblings I've been hearing around the hallways lately."

"Rumblings, sir?"

"Yes, rumblings. Perhaps about you moving?"

"Ah!" Bea smiled. "Well, yes. I am set to move, actually. But I didn't think it was newsworthy enough to tell you before filing my address changes."

"Didn't think to tell me? My dear girl, how on earth did you expect we would fill your fall courses, pray tell?"

"Oh, no, no. I'm not quitting and moving halfway around the world or anything! I'm just moving about 15 miles from here, just to the west side," Bea said with a blush.

"Oh! Well, that is a relief. Did you not just purchase a different home recently? Not that I am judging. As you know I recently moved downtown on somewhat of a whim within a mere two years of moving to St. Louis. Although it was further from campus it provided the most beautiful space for all my art," he said, looking wistful and fondling the handle of his trowel.

Bea knew all about Dean Powell's reputation for adorning his home with numerous large-breasted statues; although during her tenure she had never attended one of his nefarious parties. Rumors did run rampant in Liberal Arts, and rumors about Dean Powell's parties and his propensity to purchase student art from the nude sculpting courses (in which an unnamed female faculty member frequently modeled) was well-traversed conversational territory in their building.

"Yes, I did purchase it not that long ago, but I uh, I am newly attached," she smiled timidly, uncertain as to why she felt embarrassed. "My boyfriend has a great house on the west side of town, and Oliver and I are planning to join him there soon."

"Ah ha! The truth is revealed. So, do share. Is this someone you connected with during your final graduate studies last fall, Dr. Stanley? Am I hearing that all the time you spent at Southern U over the last several years, presumably obtaining your PhD, was actually in pursuing what has long been called an MRS degree?"

Dean Powell's grin and wink made Bea nauseous and further confirmed that, although she adored her students, her growing restlessness as a faculty member of this particular university was justified. To ensure you are the least expensive university in the state, you have to cut costs somewhere, and at Bea's school, those cost savings were usually gleaned from two places: hiring the least expensive (read: newly degreed) faculty, and taking administrative hand-me-downs who couldn't advance successfully at other state universities. Her mouth hung agape, she was frozen and amazed by his obliviously sexist condescension - not unusual, as he was infamous for his habit of "dear girl-ing" any female professor within forty years of his age - and angry with herself for again feeling hesitant to share her move details with anyone. She was also frustrated at her apparent inability to stand up and punch him square in the face.

"Um, yeah. Was there anything else, sir? I have papers to grade," Bea stood a little too quickly and knocked over his nameplate.

"No, no. It sounds like you have many life happenings. Carry on. Oh, and do let me know if there is anything we can do to assist. Perhaps recommendations for a decorator to help you spruce up your beloved's man cave."

"Oh, no, thank you," Bea said, her look laced with veiled aggression. "I'm fairly confident our styles are quite different. Have a nice day," she said, smiling weakly as she closed the door behind her.

Chapter 15

Harold and Lloyd both complained about the unusually brisk mid-April temperature as they headed toward open mic night at the Wolf Public House. The plan was for Lloyd to drop Harold off at eight for his hot date, as his beloved Miss Fisher was in the shop for its semi-annual Q-tip detailing and he called in a favor from the disastrous suit of armor incident. However, upon reaching the Wolf's parking lot, Lloyd circled for a spot.

"Umm, Daddy," jabbed Harold. "You don't need to park and walk me in to school. I'm a big boy. I can hop out without a red sign and a crossing guard, and I won't freeze to death during the 12-foot walk to the door. Bro, what the hell? I thought you were just dropping me off. I'm gonna get really pi-, uh, ticked off if you put a damper on my manly vibe."

"What? Oh, yeah, I know. I just figured since Oliver and I hadn't eaten yet, we'd pop inside. You know, grab a piece of pizza, watch you make a fool of yourself with this girl, that kind of thing. Besides, I'm guessing you'll need a ride home."

Lloyd's attempted humor just made him sound more anxious, but Harold was so caught up in his own trepidation over successfully using the newly-popular O^3 dating site he gave no indication he had noticed this about Lloyd.

Harold snorted. "Jealous much? Dude, the only thing you're going to see is the back of me as I head out the door with a hot chick in a plaid miniskirt in approximately 20 minutes. I'll be doing the jeans jackadoo before your pretty little head even hits the pillow. No ride necessary, my friend. I'll be taking my own ride," Harold said while air-humping in his seat.

Lloyd shook his head as his eyes searched the lot across the street. He continued to circle, "So what do you know about this woman, anyway?"

"All I know is she's some sort of hot co-ed, grad student maybe, who hates umbrella drinks and reality television, and by all signs is freaking hilarious and smokin' hot."

"Wait, didn't I read that the site has no pictures? How do you know she's smokin' hot, or even a co-ed? Which by the way, is like fifteen years your junior in case you forgot." Lloyd asked, circling a second time in his struggle to find a parking spot.

It was the first Friday of the month, which made it quite difficult to find an opening, but ultimately he squeezed in between a Prius and the dumpster. His tires crunched over a chunk of ice, and his entire body clenched, worried at first that it was a beer bottle.

Harold frowned at him. "Bud, just admit to being a lonely, sorry son-of-a-b-, uh, sorry Ollie!" he said over his shoulder, then, lowered his voice, "S.O.B. who wants to see what kind of mega-babes this O^3 site can serve up. Faking it doesn't suit you, sir. Thanks for the ride. Now get lost and don't walk anywhere near me. I don't want her to think I'm some lame single dad who has replaced his wife with his kid as a bar companion. Oh, wait." Harold got out and slammed the door, striding toward the entrance a little too quickly to appear calm, straightening his collar and brushing off his jacket sleeves as he walked.

Lloyd, however, was too absorbed in his own anxiety to yell insults at him, and he was thankful Harold went in ahead. It gave him time to grab his belongings unquestioned and give himself a last-minute, silent pep talk.

As Lloyd opened the rear door he breathed in deeply. "Okay, Oliver," he said excitedly. "Let's grab a bite, and, maybe listen to a song or two, and see how it goes, okay?"

"Dad, I want ham with pineapple on my half of the pizza, okay? Are we playing Mario when we get home? I found a rock in the ice. Hey, what are you doing with that box, Dad? C'mon. I'm hungry," Oliver chattered all the way to the door, only pausing to make shooting sounds as he tried to hit the dumpster with his rock.

Had anyone else been in the parking lot, however, they likely would have been too busy watching Lloyd to notice Oliver. As they walked toward the door, Lloyd was engrossed in an invisible concert, his instrument case swinging as he silently conducted and kept time with whispered beats just outside the entrance. He pulled open the door, cracked his neck, and kicked his plan into high gear.

In 1995, Lloyd and Harold were convinced they

were on the verge of fame. Perhaps it was youth, perhaps bravado. Perhaps simply too many repeat viewings of *Purple Rain.* Whatever the cause, they were sure something big was on their musical horizon. Having played together through years of high school marching band, they formed a rock band in 1993 called The Bart Chimps, as they were coincidentally both huge fans of *The Simpsons* and *The Monkees.*

Instead of trying to do well in their college coursework, they spent most afternoons snagging practice time at a local bar where Lloyd bartended three evenings a week. Their "thing" was to play Van Halen covers accompanied by elaborate light shows reminiscent of Phantom Regiment drills. Their band consisted of Harold on drums, Lloyd on bass and, on special occasions when they slipped in a Phil Collins song or two, the Casio keyboard. Realizing the need for electronic instrumentals at pubs wasn't so pressing, they eventually recruited a blond rich kid who had moved into a house two blocks from Lloyd's parents when they were all sophomores in high school. The kid's father was a packaged chicken mogul, which ensured they always had a cool warehouse (literally cold) to practice in and a nice set of functioning instruments.

Their covers weren't horrendous, so in the summer of 1995, the same time their front-man dyed his hair black and began referring to himself as Lestat, their calendars were booming with monthly gigs packed with at least thirty patrons. They were confident success was just around the corner. One Saturday in early August, however, they were mistakenly booked to play a 7pm show at a well-known gay bar, a place they'd never entered but by whom they were more than happy to be paid. As it was, when they had called to inquire about the feasibility of playing there, the waitress taking down their message wrote their name as "The Butt Chaps" and decorated their phone message with a rainbow. Suffice it to say, their covers and khakis weren't doing much to warm up the crowd before the midnight drag show, and the taunts (and at least one heartfelt, intimate offer) bothered Lloyd enough that he rapidly found excuses for not playing the next few gigs. The Bart Chimps dissolved shortly thereafter. Lestat moved to New York to pursue a full-time music career and got his big break playing piano for the first and only Marcy Playground world tour. Harold and Lloyd, however, left performing publicly for good.

That was all about to change. Lloyd's brilliant idea for winning back Bea required he re-enter the performing spotlight. A few weeks back, when experiencing his *Midnight in Paris* dream, he found himself drawn to renting Richard Linklater's *Before Sunrise* and *Before Sunset* films. Lloyd had remembered watching them both once before with Bea, and he remembered they both liked the films a lot, although he was reasonably certain they enjoyed them for diverse but not contradictory reasons. Lloyd appreciated the cinematography, which felt like one unending, unedited 24-hour shoot. He remembered Bea crying throughout several parts of each and later noting how much she enjoyed what she described as "a realistic love story, warts and all." Regardless, when he dreamed about the

Parisian bookstore, he felt the universe was sending him a signal that the last effort wasn't going to work, and at this point he believed the Linklater film provided him the surest path toward Bea.

Knowing he couldn't get anywhere trying to play a waltz on the bass, his instrument of choice throughout his stage days (and a waltz serenade was precisely what he had determined he needed to recreate from the infamous end scene from *Before Sunset*) he opted to revert to clarinet, his instrument of choice through his middle school orchestra days. He hadn't played it in any real way since that time, but for a while there he played second chair and could pull off a mean version of "Greensleeves." The fact that he could usually find Bea at the Wolf's monthly open mic night made him absolutely convinced Julie Delpy's waltz was the answer and now was the time. As it was so close to the first Friday of the month, he wasn't afforded much practice time, but he had worked up a clarinet version of the waltz he felt was passable.

Harold cocked an eyebrow confusedly when he saw Lloyd walk in holding Oliver's hand on one side and a Selmer instrument case on the other. As Lloyd and Oliver made their way toward him, Harold just shook his head and moved across the room.

"Uh, I'm going over here. Please, feel free to take my seat," he bowed and picked up his drink. "I need a clear line of sight to the front door. That way, if she's butt ugly I can duck out quickly while she's looking for me. That way, of course, I can pretend you're a stranger because, let's face it, you are strange and about to do something dumb as shit." He walked away shaking his head and chuckling, but once planted at a table across the room, he appeared visibly nervous and continually adjusted his clothing.

The smell of fresh-baked pizza and microbrews surrounded Lloyd, as did the sound of someone reading an excerpt from *Leaves of Grass,* although he couldn't see the orator. So Lloyd moved further into the restaurant and placed Oliver upon a red leather barstool on the food side of the establishment with a clear line of sight to the stage. This performance area was in a rowdier wing of the Wolf that regulars called "Eagle's Landing," primarily because it was rare to spot real talent there, but on those occasions they arrived, they were swamped by gawkers and photographers wanting to document such an endangered species. Lloyd remained as subtle as possible as he opened his clarinet case and began putting the joints together. "Ma'am, could we get a Hawaiian pizza and two lemonades, please?" he said to the bartender. "Thanks. Alright, Oliver," he said with certainty as he screwed on the mouthpiece. "Here's my phone, in case you get bored. I'll be right back. This won't take long." Before he could talk himself out of it, he quickly strode toward the stage.

After sitting with Sam for over an hour, Bea couldn't help but notice how strange he was acting. Her first thought was perhaps it was proof he wasn't quite right for her, and her second thought was it wasn't a good sign she seemed to be searching for proof of this. To be fair, Sam was acting quite peculiarly, sitting on both hands when not tapping nervously on his beer glass, repetitively looking at the clock behind the saluting Indian statue near the stage. Rather than dwell on it, though, Bea tried her hand at humorous commentary about the groups around them, such as the size of the laptop screen used by the man nearest the stage and how funny it was that he was staring at the screen rather than the performer standing three feet in front of him.

The Wolf's arrow-shaped log tables - designed as if someone cross-pollinated a mountain lodge and a Portland bike shop and then air dropped it into a Midwest strip mall – provided a lot of desk space. It was known to draw anti-establishment establishment workers each weekday. It was where the Midwestern cubicle-dwelling counter-culture itched to spend their work hours rather than chair-filling at corporate headquarters. But doing this during open mic night, to Bea, was taking virtual work environments to the extreme. She giggled as she made these comments aloud, but Sam barely smiled. Since she was convinced she was the funniest person she knew (barring Zoe), she assumed it was because he couldn't hear her over the performers and crowd, so she focused her attention on the stage.

What Bea didn't realize at the time was that Sam had been at Kastanzie's Jewelers earlier that afternoon learning what differentiates a cushion cut from a princess cut. It had been eighteen months since Sam shopped for rings there, and another eleven months prior to that. In those in-between months, he only came in to burn up some of his post-ring-return credit on the occasional new piece of crystal for his house or for wedding gifts. Whenever he dropped in, of course, he never paused to catch up on current trends in engagement rings. In fact, he did everything possible to avoid looking toward the engagement ring area of the store. When his last proposal went awry, he ended up slobbering all over the engagement ring case sharing his teary break-up story with a forbearing sales clerk who stood quietly in front of him ready to hit it with the Windex as soon as he finished. However, earlier on this particular day he had arrived at Kastanzie's ready to enter as soon as the doors opened, with store credit to burn and the conviction that Bea was indeed The One.

Sam had even stopped by the Wolf earlier that afternoon to make arrangements he believed would perfect the proposal. He had talked to the amiable owner and left a song request for anyone volunteering at the open mic: an acoustic version of PINK's "Love Song." Since performers were asked to sign into the list with a staff member prior to taking the stage, each would be asked if they would be willing to play the requested song, and the owner assured him someone would play it. When the song began, the owner would know it was time to serve up the pre-ordered heart-shaped pizza and Sam would know it was time to drop to one knee.

With each performance, Sam's nervousness amplified. Seven performers had come and gone and the song had yet to be played. As Bea sang away to covers of the Indigo Girls and swayed to some original music, Sam began to worry that it was perhaps too difficult for these performers to play the song. Tension needed to be released.

As Bea provided wild applause to an a capella duo doing a Ben Folds cover, Sam summoned all his courage and reached for Bea's hand. He missed, however, for at that moment she jerked it up to cover her mouth. She froze in shock as she watched Lloyd bypass the sign up table, nearly trip over the blooming crystal LED tree, hop directly on stage, and snap the wireless mic off the next performer's shirt, who could do nothing more than step aside, baffled and shooting irritable, quizzical looks toward the staff member who simply shrugged.

The room, at first abuzz with excitement at the a capella's cover of "Brick," quickly went silent as everyone stared at the newcomer in hopes of identifying him or, at least, catching on to what had to be an inside joke, as clarinet-wielding 35 year olds dressed like they just left a Target shift were a rarity. Lloyd's hands visibly trembled as he found the instrument's holes. He looked directly at Bea, took a deep breath, closed his eyes, and began to play.

All attention was on Lloyd. Even Sam stopped fidgeting and stared in amazement at the stage where Lloyd played his version of Julie Delpy's love waltz, eyes closed and mind focused on remembering his finger placement. This was it, his no-holds-barred rendition of a song he knew she would recognize. A blatant romantic gesture, an unabashed ode to times passed and, hopefully, love regained. He knew he had to nail this, to remember every note. This scene redo was up front, in your face. There was no way she could miss this message and there was no way it could be attributed to anyone but him.

As it turns out, he did remember his finger placements for every note. Unfortunately, he didn't remember how to *play* every note and, in his attempt to recall the note order, he failed to notice the snickering. The sound emitting from his clarinet had reached a level of atrocity unbeknownst to The Wolf. It was as if a goose was being used as a pogo stick. Harold threw his hands over his ears and looked nervously at the kayak hanging from the ceiling above his table, worried the frequency and volume might somehow split the strings and cause it to drop. He took one hand off to quickly move his beer six inches to the right.

Bea was so taken aback by the squawking that it took her a full two minutes to become aware her mouth hung open. Embarrassed, she looked around the room praying no one would have a clue that she knew the mystery musician and – please, God, no – that this song was meant for her. That's when she spotted Oliver. Her eyes narrowed furiously and she glared at Lloyd, who of course didn't see her as he had his eyes closed, deep into the moment. She jumped out of her chair and headed across the room toward Oliver's barstool.

Lloyd was nearing the end of the song when Zoe walked in, one eye squeezed shut and an index finger rubbing her ear canal. She spotted Bea and Oliver and walked over to them, then stared at the stage incredulously. She could tell how appalled Bea was by the look on her face and her rigid movements as she helped Oliver put on his jacket. "What the hell is going on?" she said into Bea's ear. "I just saw four terrified cats screaming across the car park. It sounds like a budgie trapped in a blender in here."

"No, Zoe," Bea said through gritted teeth as she zipped Oliver's jacket. "It's Lloyd. Apparently he thought it would be a brilliant idea to bring our child to a bar and then see how much public humiliation he could generate." She made eye-contact with Sam then motioned toward the door with her head. "C'mon, Ollie. Let's grab your pizza and head home. It's past your bedtime." Sam checked his pocket for the ring box, then grabbed his jacket and went to meet them at the door.

"Right," Zoe said. "Well, I'd best grab a table and a drink to calm my nerves. I was terrified when I walked in that this lovely serenade was coming from the O^3 guy I'm here to meet. Better you than me, sweetie. No offense. Bye, lovey." Zoe hugged both Bea and Oliver, waved at Sam, then walked across the room to find a table. She was unaware her path passed directly in front of Harold's table and therefore unaware of the look on his face, one of both shock and worry.

A few random claps followed the conclusion of Lloyd's song. Most seemed a result of him having reached the song's end. He slowly opened his eyes and stared directly at Bea's seat, but she was gone. He searched the room frantically and just caught the edge of her cobalt-blue coat disappearing through the front door with Oliver in tow. Lloyd jumped down and trotted after them.

Bea asked Sam to buckle Oliver into his booster seat as she saw Lloyd coming outside. She momentarily fantasized about picking up the pink metal flamingo near the entrance and smacking Lloyd across the face with it.

Instead she laid into him as soon as he walked over with the sort of muffled screaming that only parents who take their children to restaurants would understand.

"What in the hell were you thinking, Lloyd? I swear, sometimes I think you…you…ugh!" she was so angry she couldn't speak. She paced a second and kicked some gravel. The rocks flew a little too far, hitting a pair of kayak paddles the Wolf had propped by their mailbox and causing them to fall with a clatter.

"Bea! Calm down. C'mon on. I was just trying out my mad musical skills," Lloyd tried to chuckle. "Remember? You used to always tell me to go back and try playing gigs again. Just having fun, you know? Besides, it was a pretty cool cover, don't you think?" he tried to touch her arm in hopes she'd smile back at him.

"I don't have a clue what you were trying to cover but I do know you ignored the fact that Oliver hadn't eaten since his eleven o'clock school lunch and you decided to bring him to a bar. You also apparently couldn't give a rat's ass that I was here. On a date, no less," she glared at him and jerked her head toward Sam who was just closing Oliver's door.

"Oliver was fine. We had chips on the way here," Lloyd said. "We both thought it would be funny if I played here. Besides, it's a restaurant. No harm in taking him to a restaurant, right?"

Sam walked up behind Bea. "Lloyd," Sam said, extending his hand to shake Lloyd's. "That was…something…in there. You've got guts. I'll give you that."

"Yeah," Lloyd shook his hand quickly. "Listen, Bea.

I didn't do anything in some attempt to upset you. Why don't I stop by later tonight and we can talk about it? You know, after Sam drops you and Oliver off for the night?"

"I'm not interested in talking about it with you, and I'm not going home. You can call me next week to talk about Oliver's schedule," Bea said as she walked away. "Goodnight, Lloyd," she said then slammed the car door.

"Um, Lloyd, you might want to head back in. I believe you're still wearing the wireless mic," Sam said, offered a small salute, then hopped into the car as well.

Lloyd looked down at his shirt, watched them pull away, then turned slowly back toward the Wolf. At least eighteen faces were pressed against the glass watching him as he sat down dejectedly at a table outside the entrance, slowly hitting his forehead against the round wooden table top.

Chapter 16

Harold swung furiously at the bird house with his hammer in the gray-blue light of the kitchen. "Hell, yeah!" he exclaimed. "This is a great way to burn sexual frustration. Why didn't I start building shit like this years ago?" he said to Lloyd.

Lloyd sat on Harold's kitchen counter with his head hung low. He lifted his head a fraction, just enough to see Harold out of his peripheral vision, then dropped his face into his hands and groaned.

"Wait, what am I supposed to say again? This movie always freaked me out," Harold paused his banging, then started again with gusto. "Oh, yeah. You should just call the eraser guys and erase her, dude. That's what she did to you. That's what I'd do. Hey, maybe I should dump you and hang with her instead. At least she doesn't go around sobbing all the time. 'Oh, Harold! It's just not fair!'" Harold fake-sobbed and rubbed the corners of his eye. "Bea was the intelligent one in the relationship, I'm starting to notice. At least she knows when to give it up. I guarantee, unlike Kate Winslet, if Bea made it a point to erase you from her memory, she damn sure didn't do it as a lark. I'm sure she thought about it for a very long time. That shit would have been calculated and intentional." Harold tilted his head to listen as Beck's

"Everybody's Gotta Learn Sometimes" began playing on cue and filtered through the kitchen. He rolled his eyes provocatively at Lloyd and gestured toward the origin of the music.

Lloyd jumped down from the counter and started pacing the kitchen while Harold banged away. "Do you know that in the last year of our relationship she watched this movie, *Eternal Sunshine of the Spotless Mind,* like, once a month? We actually saw it during the opening weekend. She walked out of the theater and walked right back in to watch it a second time," Lloyd said, shaking his head.

Harold snorted, "Um, yeah. Like *that* wasn't a sign."

"That must be why I'm thinking about it now," Lloyd said, rubbing his forehead pacing. "No other reason to have movie sequence dreams at this point, since you and I both know the scene recreation strategy has been a complete and utter failure." He stopped walking and rested his forehead against the kitchen cabinet. "I mean, look where it has taken me. I started out in these stupid dreams as a romantic John Cusack in his physical and thespian prime and now I'm standing here as a half-deranged Jim Carrey in a movie about a brutal end to a messy relationship. Fantastic." He began pacing again, then stopped, looking incredulous as Zoe walked into the kitchen.

"For Christ's sake, Harold, will you please stop with the banging? Give it a rest. If you don't I'll be fully justified in taking that hammer and sticking it directly up your bum. Do you feel me, mate?" She walked out again with a cup of tea and a pack of Tim Tams. Lloyd looked at Harold with a "what-the-hell-was-that?" gesture.

"Don't look at me, dude. It's your dream sequence. You're the one who made her my wife in this Godforsaken fantasy," Harold said, peeking down the hallway with a fearful look as he tried to pound in the next two inch finishing nail as quietly as possible. "So, *Eternal Sunshine.* Does that mean I get to bury you in the sand or make you wear a dorky toboggan? Maybe throw little potato people at you? Stick electrodes to your head and give you a nice zzzzap?" Harold smiled a little too widely during the last comment, making an electrocution sound and choking gesture, then pounded away again.

"Funny. You're hilarious."

"You know, while we're at it, why couldn't you at least make me Mark Ruffalo, man?" Harold put the hammer down long enough to glare at Lloyd. "Can I not at least get high and have sex with Kirsten Dunst? I thought you were my friend," He carried the birdhouse to the window sill, placed it off center, and walked around it as an artist might who was considering his most magnificent masterpiece. "Of course, to be fair, David Cross is hilarious and way more critically acclaimed than you will ever be, Fake Jimbo Carrey. However, *your* pratfalls, Lloyd Stanley, are freakin' hilarious. Neither intentional nor subtle, but hilarious nonetheless. Case in point: the face plant you barely avoided while hopping onto that open mic stage at the Wolf last week. Whoo doggy! Classic." He went back to the table, picked up the hammer, and handed it to Lloyd. "Here. You'll need this in a few scenes when you have to kill that bird. Hard core, dude, but on the bright side, at least you'll get some practice wearing a cape."

"Great. Thanks," Lloyd said sarcastically, taking the hammer. "Wait, what do you mean 'get some practice?'"

"Aww, now c'mon, dude. You know what I mean. Let's take a walk down memory lane. We agreed that if you bombed miserably with this doomed-to-fail strategy to win back Bea, you'd need to hold up your end of the bet. You also heard me say repeatedly that I'd pay you back for making me run till I puked that day you were chasing her, remember? Now, you have to pay – at the Glo Run. Saturday, May 2nd. It's all you, baby. Ahh, yes, I see by the blood leaving your face that it's all coming back to you now, and since you are forced to wear whatever I tell you to, we both know you will be adorned with that most beautiful cape I handed you last week that you happened to have looked at just before you fell into this shit hole of a nightmare." Harold closed and snapped his toolbox. "Just watch out. You know what *The Incredibles* taught us about capes. Steer clear of jet engines, large fans, that sort of thing."

"Are you serious right now?" Lloyd pleaded.

"Hey, them's the rules, my friend. You made your bed and you didn't get to lay her in it. Tough but true and you still have to pay up. Nice try with the pseudo-forgetting, though," Harold put his arm around Lloyd's shoulders and steered him toward the back door. "I might guess that means the eraser guys are almost here. However, we both know you don't have enough money to write a check to Lacuna, Incorporated, so nothing to blame the memory lapse on except for your sad desire to forget the last nine months or so ever happened. Now, c'mon on. Let's head to the Charles River. I want to see how big of a bruise I can give you when I push you down on the ice."

Lloyd awoke abruptly, convinced he'd fallen into frigid water. It took him a while to realize he was still on his couch. As it happened, his alarm was set to the "forest stream" sound and he was dripping with sweat. Maybe it was depression over the open mic night catastrophe. Maybe it was simply the realization that he was about to run three miles (something he had not done since high school and, even then, not well at all). Maybe it was because he had to run it adorned with a scarlet bathing suit and cape, a fuchsia wimple and fuchsia spandex tights (something he had, of course, never done). He stared blankly into the shadows of his apartment as the spring sun moved through the afternoon sky. The racing outfit Harold selected for him rested on the coffee table, practically glowing through the plastic grocery bag in all its pink-ness.

Lloyd laughed despite himself. *In the weirdest way that outfit is very Harold*, Lloyd thought. The Scarlet Witch. Only Harold would select an *X-Men* vixen as the vehicle through which Lloyd would humiliate himself publicly. And Harold had taken great joy in giving it to him earlier in the week.

"Good day, my friend!" Harold had beamed when welcoming Lloyd into his house.

"You're uncharacteristically chipper today," Lloyd said, looking up when he walked in, convinced Harold had set up a bucket of water to fall on him when he entered.

"Au contraire. I'm always in a good mood, but particularly so when about to collect a payout," Harold beamed and slapped Lloyd hard a few times on the back, then deposited him in the living room as he walked down the hall.

Lloyd rolled his eyes and yelled after Harold. "Yeah, whatever. Let's just get this over with. What's it going to be, and why couldn't you just tell me on the phone when I called?"

Harold walked back toward him slowly with his hands behind his back. "Oh, I couldn't tell you because – and I'll say this as delicately as I can muster – you are too much of a little bitch right now to hear bad news over the phone. Too fragile. Like a delicate, fragile, little scarlet flower," Harold snickered and then dropped a plastic grocery bag into Lloyd's lap.

"What the hell is this?" Lloyd said. "And how in the world do you know what scarlet is?"

"This, my friend. This is scarlet. In fact, it's the Scarlet Witch outfit you'll be sporting while running through Forest Park during next week's Glo Run. Should make for colorful photographs and highly entertaining YouTube footage. Possibly even a great cosplay video for Comic Con this summer. We'll just have to see."

"But I'm not one to say 'I told you so,'" Harold said. "I am, however, one to say 'Way to go, dumbass. Now, pay up'."

"Yeah, yeah. I remember. But you said *Scarlet* Witch. This is fuchsia," Lloyd said, lifting a pink piece of fabric out of the bag and raising an eyebrow.

"It's scarlet."

"It's clearly fuchsia."

"It's clear that you need to stop learning about clothing shades from your girly GQ subscription and man up. I don't care what you call it, as long as you put it on and run until you hurl Gatorade or until someone stops you for your autograph, because, as you know, you will be #14 of the Sexiest Women in Comics. So you've got that going for you, which is nice. And it's scarlet *and* fuchsia. Now take your form-fitting ensemble and your inhaler and get the hell out of here. I'm expecting company."

As Harold ushered him to the door Lloyd tried to stop by grabbing the door frame, "Company? Oh, yeah. Whatever happened to your blind date, anyway? After I opened the Wolf's front door and tossed the mic back inside I left. I didn't go back until the next day to get my jacket and Selmer case, so I never got to see what she looked like or whether you'd had a drink thrown in your face within the first five minutes." Lloyd smirked.

"We, we didn't meet…per se. Let's just say I didn't find the Wolf the ideal place to 'get to know her,' if you know what I mean. Now, scram. I'm looking forward to seeing you run by sporting that on Saturday…kind of," Harold pushed Lloyd out the front door, closed it, and bolted it. He made a shooing gesture at Lloyd through the window then walked away. Lloyd had carried the bag dejectedly toward his car, tossed it on his coffee table, and forgotten about it.

Now, here it was, days later, mere hours before the

race. Unfortunately the Scarlet Witch would wait no longer. He walked to his fridge, opened a Diet Coke, and returned to stare at the bag. Sipping distractedly, he tried to think of any excuse imaginable to get out of doing the race. Coming up with nothing, he took a big swig for hydration.

"Oh, the hell with it," Lloyd said aloud. "Might as well get it over with." He snatched up the bag and finished the can on his way to the shower.

Once cleaned and dressed, he sat back down on his couch and opened the heart rate monitor he had purchased years ago when he and Bea first split up. The purchase was a gesture he hoped she'd see as a sign he could change, could become the man she wanted. He had specifically had it shipped to her house with a lame excuse that he couldn't remember his new apartment address when ordering it from work but he knew Bea's address. But he really just wanted her to know he had developed a sudden interest in running. In exercise. In being outside. In anything, really.

Lloyd sighed and went to work dressing for the race. When he found himself working up a sweat simply getting the monitor to adhere to his hairy cleavage and hiding it beneath the Scarlet Witch V-neck swimsuit, he became concerned about his ability to finish the race. In fact, he became concerned about the generosity of his health plan. Reminding himself he could always walk, he turned on the TV for distraction, hoping at least for a kind weather report. The news broadcast, however, was on commercial break. Lloyd busied himself cleaning up the monitor packaging and putting the wrapper into the costume bag, only half attuned to the TV until he slowly began to pick up on the sales pitch.

"Act now and you'll get three months of credit report monitoring at no additional charge. Worried about identify theft? Criminals today will SAY ANYTHING to get you to hand over your security details. Just ask BENNY AND JUNE Smith, a well-traveled couple from the GARDEN STATE. It took them years to clean up the credit mess that resulted from a bag lost during a recent vacation.

'We thought at first it was SERENDIPITY, that'd we'd received prize money and a free return vacation to Europe. All they asked for were a few minor details. Then our bank called to say our account was being used at MIDNIGHT IN PARIS. Unfortunately, it was just BEFORE SUNSET and we were in Florida, the SUNSHINE state, stranded with no idea of what was happening with our account. If only we or someone like CREDIT EXPERTS had been monitoring the transactions on the account."

Lloyd muted the TV and blinked rapidly. He shook his head a few times as if working to get water out of his ear canal and sat blinking again. *There is no way,* he thought, *that I just heard what I heard.* He reversed the program on his remote and watched the last 30 seconds of the credit monitoring infomercial again. *Serendipity? Benny & Joon? Before Sunset? Could it be that obvious? Could all of those dreams have simply been my subconscious hearing movie names in infomercials while I slept on the couch? That's it? No destiny? No epiphanies?* He reversed and watched again, twice.

Impossible. No, it had to be more. It was clearly more. He watched yet again, and again. Then, it struck him. *Perhaps,* he swallowed excitedly. *Could my subconscious – no, the universe – have been directing me toward…transaction monitoring?* Unbelievable, but it seemed to be true. *The very thing Harold suggested months ago? No way. Not possible. I must still be half asleep.*

He turned off the TV, shook his head violently, and stared at the blank screen. Then he turned to look at the clock. About an hour to sunset, which, today, meant race time. As his eyes were making their way back toward the blank screen, he noticed his laptop charging near the clock, the VPN dongle occasionally reflecting in the battery light. On those rare days he had to work remotely, that VPN dongle gave him access to data. On this day, that VPN dongle could give him access to Bea.

Could it be, he thought again incredulously, *that Harold was right all along? That the answer to connecting with Bea was to find the answer within her transactions? To analyze and predict her next moves? To uncover what was important to her at the moment? To know where she was going next? Was this the Baader-Meinhoff phenomenon in action? Was this the Police's Synchronicity in the flesh?*

Lloyd jumped off his couch and paced in front of his computer. He reached toward it, paused, reached toward it, paused, and paced again. He closed his eyes and recalled Bea's angry face in the Wolf's parking lot. Then he suddenly thought of Sam standing near Bea by his car. And Sam looking shifty and sweaty at the table with her prior to Lloyd's performance. And again, greeting him awkwardly the day they moved the armor. *That's it,* Lloyd thought. *Sam is it. Sam is the answer.*

He grabbed the computer off its charging station, plopped down on his couch, and opened the lid. *I don't have to look into Bea's personal information,* Lloyd thought. *I'll just see what Sam is doing, see if I can find anything suspicious to warn her about. Child pornography purchase receipts. Tickets to see Nickelback or something. At least if I can get him out of the picture I stand a remote chance of spending more time with her. More time to really pay attention to what makes her tick. More time to redeem myself.*

Lloyd logged into his work account and began to dig. Data mining was his specialty, so he had no doubt he could locate the information. It would then be a matter of piecing together what he saw into some sort of coherent behavior pattern and then determining what to do about the knowledge. Lloyd's level of dedication alone would ensure he could piece together a believable story about how he came across the information, and, of course, it would be significant enough he knew she would forgive the privacy invasion. Of this, he was confident.

He plugged away as the minutes ticked by. Then Lloyd's expression soured. He clicked a few more times, his eyes racing across the screen. He looked straight ahead and slowly closed his computer lid. A jewelry store. A florist. A pre-payment to a beachside condo next week. *Oh. Shit.* Lloyd realized. *He's going to ask her to marry him, possibly as early as tomorrow. That's when*

Bea was going to bring Oliver by and take a week's vacation (presumably with Sam). This is it, he thought. *The finale.*

Lloyd leaned back and closed his eyes. No more chances with Bea. How could there be? He visualized Oliver in a handsome tux walking her down the aisle and he felt nauseous. Just earlier this school year he and Bea had cracked a few jokes and shared a coffee at one of Oliver's music shows, and now she's going to marry someone else. Lloyd curled up in a ball on his couch and groaned.

Then, suddenly, he sat bolt upright. A proposal tomorrow. That meant he still had tonight. He jumped up and paced again in front of his coffee table. Tonight, tonight, tonight. *No movies, movies are out,* he thought. *This had better be original and it had better be good.* His pace increased. *Tonight... tonight...tonight.* He caught himself singing the Genesis song and smacked his face. *She likes flowers, but that's not going to make enough of an impact. Anyone can give flowers. This has to stand out. This has to be the ultimate attempt.* He paused briefly as he considered creating a mix CD, as he knew how much she adored them. But, again, he was convinced that wouldn't grab nearly enough attention, and he usually had to rely on Harold to make CDs he could give her. Besides, if she was still furious with him, it was too easy for her to just chuck it out without playing it. As he paced he glanced out the window and was briefly distracted by a bird flying across the pink sky. Lloyd froze in his tracks remembering the heartfelt message he had left on Bea's voicemail a few months ago.

That's it. Unique. Impactful. Not borrowed. Totally me. I left her the voicemail about the sunset and the birds because I wanted her to know I think of her when I see beautiful things. She deserves that much beauty, that much love. She deserves to be enveloped by beauty, by 10,000 pink birds of love swirling all around her. And that, Lloyd thought, *is what I can give her tonight.* Lloyd immediately jumped into action. He snatched his keys and wallet off the counter and tore out of the house. The race completely slipped his mind, as did the fact that he was still wearing his racing outfit. Lloyd broke every speed limit between his apartment and Hobby Lobby, just a block down from the library. He parked between the two and speed-walked toward the store, thankful for, but not cognizant of, the fact that he was wearing running shoes. He was simply worried Hobby Lobby would close any second.

At that precise moment, Veronica happened to be locking the library doors and saw Lloyd speed-walking down the other side of the street. She stopped turning the lock, stared at him confusedly, and giggled. "Hey, Stan Lee!" she yelled. "Hey, what's with the fuchsia get-up?"

Lloyd, however, was so engrossed in his mission he didn't hear her and continued at his frantic pace.

"Hey, Lloyd Stanley! Are you doing a scavenger hunt or something?" Veronica finished locking the door and turned to jog across the street to meet him, but she had to wait for a passing car.

By the time it was gone Lloyd's cape had disappeared through the store's automatic doors. Veronica smiled toward the store, thinking about how close his cape was to getting caught and wondered what he was up to. He seemed to be in too much of a hurry, however, to talk now, since he still had the library's only copy of *Before Sunset* checked out on his account, she knew she'd see him again soon. At least then she could ask about the hobby dash and the costume, even if she would have preferred grabbing dinner with him tonight to hear the details. She sighed lightly, grinned, and walked toward her car.

It took Lloyd less than 45 minutes to grab his items and return home. He walked into his kitchen and dumped the contents of the hobby store's bag on the table. Packages of pink paper, scissors, and glue bottles spilled out across the surface. He threw open the doors under his kitchen sink, grabbed two trash bags, whipped them open, and hooked them over the edges of his dining room chair. Lloyd glanced quickly at the clock, sat down, clapped once, and rubbed his hands together. He had less than three hours to make lots of birds, bag them up, drive to the bridge, and get them to Bea. Time to get to work.

Chapter 17

It was incredibly dark by the time Lloyd left his apartment. Although he had hoped to make thousands of birds for Bea, he managed to make just under 100. After making the first five, he realized 10,000 simply wasn't attainable by any human, so he opted to glue two pieces of paper together per bird to increase the wingspan. Lloyd convinced himself that fewer, larger birds would make as much, or more, of an impact as 10,000 smaller ones. Mostly, though, he was grateful he knew how to make paper birds at all.

Lloyd made his first paper bird approximately six years earlier when Bea was pregnant with Oliver. For a shower gift they had received a quirky *Oodles of Origami for Parents* book from Zoe. One night while he and Bea watched television, he decided to try his hand at creating elaborate paper airplanes and made several throughout the evening. By the time Bea went to take a bubble bath to soothe her aching back Lloyd was ready to try something else. He chose to make her a delicate turquoise bird out of paisley paper. He even glued on tiny pink peppercorn eyes before placing it on her pillow and reading a magazine in bed. When she emerged from the bathroom rubbing her hair with a towel she saw the bird and was delighted. Her face glowed and her eyes sparkled. She scooped the delicate bird in her hands, peered into its face for nearly a full minute, then set it gently down on her night stand where it remained for months. Bea cuddled up next to Lloyd and fell asleep nestled into his arm, something she never did. Bea was a don't-touch-more-than-my-fingertips kind of sleeper, even post-coitus. Lloyd went to sleep that night smiling and happy.

Tonight, however, with each crease of the paper birds, Lloyd berated himself for only making her one bird throughout the entirety of their relationship. *That little gesture had brought her so much joy*, he thought. Why did he waste that opportunity to make her happy again and again and again? More than once he had to stop folding, take a deep breath, and refocus. The self-loathing had to wait. Time was running out and he needed to funnel all of his energy into finishing the project at hand.

With 50 minutes to spare Lloyd shook down and tied the bulging garbage bags o' birds and carried them toward the front door. On the way he spotted several of Bea's kayak straps and bungee cords in his hall closet. Somehow they had mistakenly been tossed into his packing boxes when the house sold during the divorce. Lloyd never told Bea he had them. Not out of malice; more out of need to treasure them like a security blanket. He grabbed them now, thinking they might come in handy, and threw them, the garbage bags, and a movie theatre gift card into his Malibu.

With reasonable certainty, Lloyd knew where she

would be and when she would be there. Bea went to the same place every year the final weekend of the semester, without fail. Barnhart Industries. She and her students held some sort of shindig there every first Saturday of May. He couldn't remember how it began or why. Something about stories. Maybe writing stories for their website? He couldn't recall the particulars, but he knew the university paid her each year so she and her students could spend time there, and they always had a big gathering the Saturday after final exams. Bea had told him it helped Barnhart and it helped them to revel in the fact that their projects were officially over. He never went, but he knew Bea went every year.

Lloyd also knew that following the celebration Bea would do two things: drive home via the backroads, and, once home, have a Glenfiddich single malt Scotch on the rocks while burning all her student papers from the previous semester in a fire pit on her back deck, which she said helped her get through the current end-of-semester grading. Given a choice, and even a smidge of free time, Bea always chose back roads to interstates, regardless of how much it increased her travel time. She rolled her windows down, let her fingers surf the wind, and sang. She revelled in taking in all the country sights, "goose-necking" as she called it. Bea loved to drive in the country, especially, he recalled, at the beginning or the end of something. These details Lloyd knew he could count on, and that meant he knew where he should place himself to share the birds with Bea.

Driving at a rapid clip he did reasonably well with the directions, although he had only heard of the place and had never been there. He only took one wrong turn down Randy Lane, which, strangely enough, he remembered was where Bea got lost years earlier. All in all it took Lloyd just under 25 minutes to arrive at Barnhart Bridge. That meant he was able to repeat Dylan's "Make You Feel My Love" about nine times before he reached his destination.

Lloyd pulled his car over just ten feet shy of the bridge railing, near the trees by the first bald eagle pillar, and parked. Barnhart Bridge was approximately three quarters of a mile from Barnhart Industries headquarters. During World War II hundreds of local women worked tirelessly for months at that very site, which at the time was an empty lot. Under canvas tents they sewed bedding emblazoned with American flags and eagles to send abroad, as well as to sell for the troops. They were so successful and well-organized that after the war several remained together and created one of the first women-owned textile factories, Barnhart Industries, which still produced patriotic clothing and accessories.

In order to pay tribute to these pioneering women and the money and jobs they brought to Imperial, Missouri, the city erected an ornate metal bridge at the intersection of Old Ferry Road and Highway M sometime in the early 1980s. It was replete with bald eagles adorning the piers, girders, handrails, and parapet. Lloyd knew Bea had to drive under this exact bridge to make her way back toward the city on Highway M, and he knew her celebration was scheduled from seven to nine o'clock every year. Confident in this knowledge, he climbed out and reached into his trunk for the bird bags and gear.

It wasn't until the cold wind whipped at his lycra leggings that he realized he was still dressed as the Scarlet Witch. Lloyd's face flushed. He paused, gripping the trunk lid, cursing. He tried to brainstorm alternatives for a few seconds, but ultimately he knew it was much too late to go and grab new clothing. He had about ten minutes left and he had to make the most of it, Scarlet Witch or no Scarlet Witch.

Lloyd slammed the trunk and carried his trash bags and accessories toward the railing. While making birds the thought had occurred to him that he'd better have a plan in place as to what to do if – or, as he liked to think, *when* - Bea found this supreme gesture endearing. He briefly thought about bringing a pup tent with him as he loaded the car, in case she wanted to stay there, camp in the peaceful surroundings, and reconnect. Since Lloyd's mother had plans with Oliver, they'd have some flexibility.

Barnhart Industries was near the Historic Bridge State Park, so it was indeed wooded and serene. However, since he had no pup tent, had never owned a pup tent, and had no hope of putting a pup tent up in the dark, he decided against it. Lloyd also wasn't much of a drinker, and he figured bar-hopping that early into a renewed relationship would likely cause an old, habitual argument to surface. He was also afraid of inviting himself back to Bea's house. Too domestic-y for just after reconnecting. It would scare her away. But he knew she found it very, very difficult to say no to any invitation to the movies, even those she received from mere acquaintances or near-nemeses. So a light-hearted, late-night movie date seemed an apropos solution, which is why he had opted to bring his movie gift card.

Hugging the nearest post, he peered down past an eagle's wing at Old Ferry Road below. Three of the four street lights around the bridge were functioning, so the bridge itself was reasonably well-lit. But it was pitch black under the bridge and along the exterior, as the only light to be found was coming from a farmhouse 400 yards away. It seemed the kind of road never heavily trafficked during the day, and at night likely long stretches of time would pass before any car traversed it. It was unusually cold for early May, still a fair bit above the record low of 34 but abnormally cold nonetheless. There was no movement whatsoever. Lloyd could see well enough past the adjacent clump of trees to note there were no lights on at nearby Firehouse #2, and the limestone cliffs surrounding the bridge added to the sense of isolation.

Good. That gives me the opportunity to position myself without drawing attention or inciting an unwanted 911 call from a passerby who might think I'm jumping. He got to work.

He grabbed the icy-cold handrail with one hand and the straps of the garbage bags with the other. After a long pause prompted by the suspicion that he might be having a heart attack, Lloyd ultimately convinced himself his fear of losing Bea had to trump his fear of heights. He took several deep breaths in and out, momentarily watching them hang in the air, then began scuttling along the exterior ledge toward the bridge's center. The

18 inch platform felt more like three, but Lloyd knew logically there was plenty of room for him to stand flat footed with his back to the bridge. *Slow and steady, slow and steady.* He began to shuffle slowly along the cold, damp edge of the bridge.

Once halfway across, he set the bags down on the interior side and turned toward the handrail. He used both hands to wrap the heavy duty straps around the handrail and himself multiple times. He couldn't recall much from his few years in Boy Scouts, but he did recall how to tie a rolling hitch knot. In the unlikely event he remembered incorrectly, though, he had also grabbed four bungees. He wrapped those around the railing, too. He also tied two of the hooks to the straps, one he cinched multiple times around his waist, and the last he knotted into his cape. Lloyd didn't plan to need any of them, of course, but he assumed in this instance it was better to be safe than splattered and sorry. After yanking on the straps several times and feeling assured he was well tethered, he grabbed both bags and pivoted around. Lloyd's body faced outward and he got a true bird's eye view of Old Ferry Road. He squinted and could easily see the cars parked outside the Barnhart building. All there was left to do was wait.

There was no doubt he knew *what* to do. As for the *when* Lloyd also felt fairly confident. First of all, he believed Bea would likely be one of the last to leave the celebration. Not dead last, as that would have to be the facility owners themselves, but near last. Second, he had 20/20 vision, even in the dark. He had never needed glasses, even as he got older. Unlike his muscle tone or heart rate, this at least gave him something physical to brag about regularly. Therefore, he knew he would be able to see the distinctive green glow of her headlights approaching. He was convinced he'd be able to tell precisely when it was time to let the birds fly.

Cars began to leave Barnhart Industries one by one as Lloyd waited and watched. It was difficult to be patient perched at that height enveloped in those chilly temperatures. A few moments in, he mentally acknowledged he should have embraced Bea's suggestion a few years back that she buy him a nice watch for their anniversary. He had dismissed the idea at the time, as he always relied on his phone for the time and saw no justification for doing otherwise. But tonight there had been nowhere for him to put his phone except into his Scarlet Witch swimsuit. He obviously had no pockets. Now, as the phone slowly slid its way uncomfortably down the front of his torso, he regretted that decision. Lloyd tried a few times to reach down the front of the suit to retrieve it, but each time he felt unstable and grasped the railing in fear. The phone felt sticky, bulging low and uncomfortably on his abdomen, and there was no way to determine exactly what time it was or when the celebration officially ended. Lloyd was left to wait, watch, and count the remaining cars in the parking lot. Once four cars remained, Lloyd tensed. His breathing shallowed in anticipation.

A millennia of arguments about fate and destiny preceded this moment and no doubt a millennia would follow. Some spiritual philosophers believe humans are fated to play character roles in series of events put in play by a much larger, more powerful being, that we humans are meant to live lives mostly beyond our control. Others have long argued that, although we may be destined for certain events, failures, and successes, our ultimate destiny lies within our own hands, that our chosen actions craft our consequences. It is likely that the truth lies somewhere in a gray area between these polarities.

Lloyd never fancied himself a fatalist. Therefore, when reflecting on this night and where his life went thereafter, he imagined for decades what would or could have been had he made this or that minor shift in action. Bea, on the other hand, considered herself a proactive, Pollyanna. Whenever the moment of the birds and the bridge entered her mind over the years, she tended to believe that what happened that night was meant to be.

Perhaps it was fate that called that night. Perhaps destiny. Regardless, at precisely the moment Lloyd squinted down the dark highway and recognized Bea's car making its way toward the bridge, Harold definitely called. In fact, he called Lloyd's phone, and, getting no answer and wanting to know why Lloyd was a no-show at the race, called again thrice more. Unfortunately, Lloyd's phone, which received all three calls, was turned to both a Beastie Boys' "Sabotage" ring tone and vibrate.

The vibration, of course, quickly became the primary concern, because Lloyd's phone at his point had worked its way from the top of the Scarlet Witch swimsuit, past his abdomen, and into his crotch. The vibrations emanating from this precarious place startled Lloyd so much that he jerked his arms inward, whereas he had been holding them wide to let the birds out of their bags, and immediately looked down at his crotch. He danced his body around quickly to ease the discomfort and shift the phone's position. But as he did, he began to wobble, and because he was looking downward, he did not see or hear the rapidly approaching truck full of teenagers rolling down the road playing mailbox baseball. Therefore, whatever imbalance had begun by the phone's ringing amplified as Lloyd heard the whooping and hollering kids in the F-150 take a bat to his Malibu's side mirror.

The crunching metal sounded like an explosion. Lloyd whipped his head up to see what was happening, thus causing him to completely lose his footing. He flung the trash bags into the air in fright, and his arms flailed toward the handrail, but it was too late. The distance between his hands and the railing was too great, and as the teenagers barrelled across the bridge and on down the highway oblivious to his existence, Lloyd dropped toward the road below. *Shit. So this is how it ends,* he thought. *A crowd of gawkers, a freezing wind, a lost love, and, me dangling 30 feet above the parkway.*

Of all nights to be wearing pink lycra.

Typically Lloyd's over-preparedness was seen by others as a desperate act of anxiety. In this rare moment, however, it's the only thing that saved him. Three of the straps and bungees held, and Lloyd found himself saved, albeit dangling, 30 feet above the road below. He bobbed up and down like a puppet, one arm in the air and his back flat as if he were flying. Frozen in fear, he had clamped his eyes shut tightly on the descent. When he could finally bring himself to open them, he saw three cars through the flock of birds circling round his head. One had apparently been passing under him as he fell and it had swerved off the road in a panic. He could see the skid marks under the bridge. Another was directly below him. The third car, slowly pulling to a stop just before the bridge, was Bea's.

Bea's car stopped approximately 20 yards from the bridge and moved slowly toward the shoulder. He could see her blond hair through the front windshield. He could see her pause for what seemed to him like eternity before putting her Acura in park. He heard yelling and cursing from the other two cars, and, within moments, sirens in the distance. With his free hand, he covered his eyes and felt his heart sink, as the last of the paper birds floated past him on its descent to the road below.

Chapter 18

It took Bea a bit to wrap her mind around what she was seeing. A human toy dangling by strings above the road. A marionette of the gods. A marionette whose name she happened to know: Lloyd. She slowly brought her car to a full stop and stared upwards for a long while. Then she slowly pulled over to the shoulder and turned down Garth Brooks' "To Make You Feel My Love." She'd had it cranked up after leaving Barnhart Industries, and she sat for a while longer listening to it and watching the chaos unfold.

The farm hand who had swerved in a panic when the objects came flying down from the bridge was standing beneath Lloyd. He was shaking his fist up at him and shouting. After a stream of obscenities, he kicked a bird that floated by his foot and went to sit inside his truck until the police arrived. The two students who had departed just moments before her, Aaron and his girlfriend Megan, were directly below the bridge. They jumped out of the car to see what in the world they had driven into, and they seemed to be arguing. There was also a truck-load of teenagers reversing down the road to park near the bridge. They hopped out of the back of the pickup, laughing and occasionally yelling "Whoa!" and "Dude!" Bea slowly turned off her engine and rested her head on the steering wheel trying to sort through the range of emotions coursing through her at that moment. As she was preparing to climb out she heard Megan and Aaron shouting at one another.

"Baby, I kid you not. This was totally unplanned madness. Like, a freak accident or something," Aaron pleaded.

"Who the hell is the dude in the tights? Do you know this guy? Because it seems awfully convenient that Pinky there dropped right in front of your car like a present out of Santa's bag. Like he was waiting for you or something. Have you been using your real name on the Manties sites again? Or, is this, like, some frat hazing your buddies at Delta Sig have gotten you into now? Jerks." Megan may have been asking Aaron, but her voice was loud and her words were spoken toward Lloyd, who hung helplessly far above the road.

"Yeah, hi!" Lloyd yelled from his upside-down position. "Sorry about that. I have no idea who that young man is. My name is Lloyd. Lloyd Stanley. And this was all just an accident. A really, really unfortunate accident," he said, softer. "Look, sorry for any inconvenience. You folks can all just go about your business. I believe I hear sirens coming this way. They can get me down, so I'm good. It's all good. I'll be fine as soon as the fire fighters arrive," Lloyd said, wincing in embarrassment. He hoped they would all simply drive away. Even Bea, at this point. And he prayed to God this rescue fell outside of Sam's jurisdiction.

"Wait, did you say Stanley? Like, as in Professor Stanley? Oh, this is PERFECT!" Megan whipped around angrily and punched Aaron in the arm. "You ass! I KNEW you had some fling going with that skanky ho," Megan jerked her thumb toward the Barnhart building they just left, "and now, here's her husband out here assuming you'll be hitting on her tonight and he's trying to drive you off the road out of jealousy! Try to tell me nothing's happening when I know goddamn well-" Megan continued to rant as she paced in circles and started messaging from her phone, pausing only for an occasional, louder tirade "-and SHE! Oh, SHE tried to tell the dean-" followed by more mumbled raving and ranting. Aaron's occasional, interjected denials were met with more arm punches and increased volume.

"Whatever!" she finally yelled at Aaron. "Just get me the hell out of here. Take me back to Tammy's so she and I can keep me from losing a perfectly good Saturday night. Piss on all of you losers!" Megan said while pulling lip gloss out of her purse.

She put some on, then flipped off Lloyd, flipped off Bea- who was slowly walking toward them- and just to ensure she got her point across, flipped off the farm hand. Then she walked back to Aaron's car, punching his arm once again as she passed by and climbed back in.

"Wait, babe!" Aaron hollered after her as he trotted toward his car. "'Sup," he said to Bea, waggling his eyebrows, then climbed into the driver's seat and continued pleading with Megan as they pulled away.

Bea shook her head, and her walking slowed as she found herself directly under Lloyd. Lloyd searched her face, which was expressionless and still. He desperately racked his brain for the right words, but he had absolutely no idea what to say, and he was slightly concerned that if he chose the wrong ones she'd throw something up at him. Her shoe, or perhaps her dinner.

But suddenly Bea grinned. Then her face broke into a wide smile. Then she began to laugh, loudly and boisterously. The watching farm hand mumbled more obscenities and peeled off down the road in his truck, ranting to himself about crazy folks from the suburbs and the full moon. Lloyd at first thought too much blood had rushed to his head, that perhaps he was imagining things, as he had already steadied himself for a swift slap in the face. However, Bea's laughter was loud and genuine.

"Oh, man," she doubled over. "That has got to be the funniest thing I've seen all year." She aimed her phone and took a picture, then wiped the corners of her eyes. "I mean, you really went off the deep end. What the hell are you doing here? And why in the world are you, well, pink? And stuck?"

A sudden wave of love and relief washed over Lloyd. "I'm, I tried…I don't even know where to start."

"How about the beginning? It sounds like the fire trucks are at least three or four miles away. Go for it, dude," Bea said, smiling. "I can barely wait to hear this."

Smiling despite his predicament, Lloyd took a breath and began telling Bea all about the dreams he had, how he had hoped to recreate moments from her favorite films to bring her joy and happiness, to bring spontaneity and love into her life, to keep her from marrying the wrong person. He told her about John Cusack and Johnny Depp, about spending midnight in Paris and pacing the kitchen like Jim Carrey. He went through each plan and each unplanned result. Bea craned her neck to listen and occasionally had to rotate to see his face, since he slowly spun in a circle. She was flabbergasted but listening intently.

"You mean, the note in the book was from you? Oh my god," she put her hand to her forehead. "I narrowly avoided a written reprimand at work over that." She shook her head and smiled.

"Yeah, I hoped you'd find it, you know, like the book John Cusack searched for in *Serendipity*. I was trying to be romantic and subtle, so…so that you'd be feeling romantic and start thinking about me," he looked away and blushed, although Bea was unaware as his face remained perpetually flushed from the blood flow. "You know, kind of a love-by-association thing." Lloyd flushed again as he saw at least ten rescue workers arrive in a variety of emergency vehicles. However, he felt he and Bea were connecting, so he continued as they began pulling tools out. "And the time you saw me with a banged-up face? I was trying to walk over a chair like Johnny Depp in *Benny & Joon*. I also tried to get a suit of armor like Sheldon in *Garden State*, but, let's just say that didn't work out so well."

Bea slapped her forehead. "The suit of armor! Right! That makes so much more sense now. I couldn't understand any of what Sam was telling me about you doing Dungeons & Dragons or something like that near Forest Park. Wow. And I remember how strange it seemed when I met you out running that day. What movie was that supposed to be from?"

"That wasn't a movie," Lloyd said abashedly. "That was just me trying to see what you were doing…and being out of shape. And it's the reason I'm dressed the way I am. Harold told me he'd pay me back for that unplanned sprint." He displayed his outfit with his hands. "I was supposed to be at the Glo Run tonight, and I'm sure Harold is driving up and down the race route hoping to find me puking and humiliated on a curb somewhere."

Bea laughed. "Okaaay. Well, what in the world was the ridiculous clarinet serenade about?" she snickered. "Were you trying to serenade me from the stage like Tom in *500 Days of Summer*?"

"Oh, no. I specifically steered clear of movies where the couple, you know," he swallowed, "didn't end up together. I was trying to play you a waltz, like Julie Delpy did in *Before Sunset*, you know, when she was making it impossible for Ethan Hawke to leave her. Aahh!!" Lloyd let out an uncontrollable yelp when one of the firefighters pulled on a bungee from the top of the bridge, causing him to drop another inch.

The rescue workers shook their heads and went back to the truck for the trauma shears and inflatable cushion.

Bea stopped snickering and stared at him. "You…you really made a lot of plans, didn't you? I don't know what to say…"

Lloyd took advantage of the opening. "You can say you feel the same way I do, that we should never have split up, that we're meant to be together, that…that Oliver is better off with us back together and working things out. That you and I are better off. C'mon, Bea.

Can't you see how much I care about you? I've changed. I have! I mean, look at me! I'm terrified of public humiliation, heights, and…well, now spandex and also cell phones. But, I did it all, I'd do anything, just to be with you. I know you love risks and romance and adventures, and I can give you all of that. Just give us another chance. Please, Bea." Lloyd looked at her hopefully, stopped talking, and waited.

Bea stared at him for a moment, took a deep breath in, and sighed. Then she tilted her head and smiled at him, "You know, you're absolutely right, Lloyd. I do love love. I love romance. I love risk and adventure. I love party tricks like walking over chairs and I love love notes left in books, scavenger hunts for soulmates, serenades, and all the rest."

Lloyd grinned broadly, and he hoped all the love he felt in his heart shone through his gaze.

"But," she paused and scuffed her shoe into the road, "I love when *I* do them."

Lloyd looked confusedly at her. "But…what? I don't understand."

"You're right. You did pay attention to all those things I love, but you never stopped to think much about *why* I love them. Hell, until recently, I really didn't either." Bea walked in circles, gesturing desperately as if grasping for the right words in the air. "I love movies like *500 Days of Summer* and *Serendipity* for the same reason: because I admire the gumption and take-no-prisoners attitude of both the Summer character and Sara in *Serendipity*. The great thing about the note in the book scene is that she didn't just jump in bed with John

Cusack, regardless of how hot he was. She was protecting her life, her career. I really admire that. I've struggled with that my whole life, thinking I can't be happy without a man in my life asking for me on his schedule and his terms. Thinking I have to be needed and be by-the-book to be happy."

Lloyd's smile slowly dropped. The rescue team had turned off all the sirens, and he stared at the silent, flashing lights while he listened.

"I love both Benny's and Joon's characters because they don't worry about what other people think. They are individually spontaneous, creative, slightly disturbed – yes – but fully present in each moment. Not because they are in love. Not at all." Bea rubbed her temples. "I love *Harold & Maude* because I secretly want to be like Maude, bold and unapologetic, living my life on my terms and not constantly working to get the gold star, the rubber stamp of approval from others. I love *Before Sunrise* and *Before Sunset* because the dialogue is more like real life. They say unkind things to each other, they make mistakes, but they're hopeful for their futures, together or apart, and they seem to simply be grateful they shared great experiences together. Plus, Julie Delpy's character stubbornly refuses to back down, even when she's making those mistakes. I admire that, I guess, because I struggle with it so much." Bea swallowed hard and used her middle fingers to wipe tears off the edges of her eyes. She stopped pacing and stared at Lloyd, her voice lowered. "It's who I'm not, but often wish I was. I don't want to need the classic 'happy ending', you know?"

Lloyd looked down the road and hoped Bea assumed it was gravity, not this disclosure, that made him teary-eyed.

"And, most of all, I adore *Eternal Sunshine of the Spotless Mind* because I like being reminded that there aren't any happiness guarantees and sometimes you have to go in knowing you will likely lose when you think the experience is worth it. Like I did with us, Lloyd." Bea took a deep breath. "The thing is, Lloyd, it's not you," Bea said kindly. "It's me. It has taken me quite a while to figure out that I want all of the things you mentioned – love, romance, adventure, risk – but I want to create them for myself. I used to think I could only find those things through a relationship in order to be happy, that to feel love I had to show love to whatever guy I was with – you included – and they would bring those things to me. For a long time I thought that to experience adventure I needed to plan elaborate outings for the men in my life. And that meant I jumped into a lot of relationships looking for it, ours included. And I'm sorry if our relationship brought you anything but happiness, but the truth is I just need to go create my own happiness, my own adventure, take my own risks. Be on my own." She laughed. "Bea on her own. You know?"

"So, how does your new 'commitment' to Sam fit into that equation?" Lloyd couldn't help but sound angry and sarcastic through his hurt, and he stared at the lights, refusing to look at her. "I can tell you this much, Bea. If he tries to interfere with my time with Oliver or you guys try to relocate or something, we're going to have a problem." Lloyd attempted to scowl, but it wasn't a natural or comfortable look for him and he merely looked like he was pouting.

Bea looked at him quizzically, wondering if there was some way he could have known Sam had just proposed to her the night before. She shook it off, "I have no commitments to anyone other than Ollie and myself. He's the only man in my life and likely will be for a while. Ollie is all the man I have room for right now," she said staring at him. "Sam is," she paused, "a great guy, and I've been lucky to have a lot of great guys in my life. You included, Lloyd," Bea smiled. "But, all of those relationships from my past have led me to this positive point in my life, and I'm moving forward. No more hanging on or looking back, for either of us. I want to see how great my life can be when I'm driving it. And now you can do the same," she smiled and looked up and down his bungees. "I mean, just look at you. You're fearless now, man! You can go wherever you want with whomever you want. And as long as we both support each other's happiness, Ollie can't help but thrive." Bea smiled softly at Lloyd, and he couldn't help but return it. "And when the time comes for us to have new partners, I have no doubt we can work through it together."

They stared at each other a few seconds, then they both looked over Bea's shoulder at the rescue workers approaching with the inflatable cushion and shears. "I have to ask, though," Bea said, "what movie was this bridge jumping from?" She gestured to the ropes and bungees and smiled. "I honestly can't recall seeing anything quite like this."

"Oh, no, this wasn't from a movie. It was just my

way of trying to…make a statement," Lloyd said shyly. "I wanted to share something of me with you." He looked toward a pile of paper birds near Bea's feet and she followed his gaze.

She picked one up.

"Well, now you're on to something. Keep that in mind next time you want to woo some sweet, less-needy girl off her feet. Speak from your heart, be yourself, and although you'll still feel terrified when you fall," Bea gently touched the paper bird's beak, "you can't lose." She stepped aside as the firefighters approached and began talking with Lloyd. One rescuer took down Bea's witness information while the others worked to release Lloyd from his tangled trap.

After 10 minutes of careful work they successfully snipped the lines and Lloyd bounced onto the cushion then onto the pavement. The lead rescuer helped him up, ensured he was coherent, then asked him to take a moment to gather his thoughts before he called his ride (Lloyd had given them Harold's number) and sat with him to complete a report.

Lloyd stared at Bea wistfully, "I hate not being with you and Oliver every day."

"I know," Bea said with her arm through his, walking him to sit and gather himself by the side of the road. "But you deserve more than I am willing to give." She smiled at him and patted his back. "And you can see Oliver every day if we can work it out. This is the 21st century! Modern families and all that. I'm not interested in following social norms and expectations anymore, remember?"

Lloyd couldn't help but grin back at her.

"Besides, if it's okay with you, I'd like to split the summer 50-50 with you this year. I need to spend some time checking the world out, battling windmills and what not. Zoe and I are planning a road trip." They grinned at each other. "Working together – not being together – is the best thing for Oliver. And for us. Are you up for it?"

Lloyd wrapped the blanket tighter around his shoulders and stared down the road. He breathed in, tipped his head for a split second toward Bea's shoulder, then breathed out strongly. "Sure. Why not? Who knows? Maybe I'll find something to battle for myself."

They both paused, taking in the moment in mutual comfort. As Bea saw Harold approaching the scene, they both stood up. "Well, that's my cue," she said, turning to face him. "Goodbye, Lloyd." She touched one cheek and kissed the other. Smiling, she gave his cheek a slap. "I'll see you, Lloyd. Enjoy your week with Ollie, and enjoy your newfound ballsy-ness. Put it to good use." As she opened her door, she turned toward the rescue workers, "Boys, he's all yours." Then she saluted Harold, climbed in her car, and drove away.

Chapter 19

Lloyd smiled as his fingers touched the Doctor Who DVDs. He hadn't noticed before how rich in geeky fodder the library's shelves actually were. Since he wasn't in an obsessive state of mind this time, he was able to take his time and take in the wonders that were the Chesterfield Public Library. Yet, although he really was taking in the titles, he was also sneaking glances toward the checkout desk. Upon catching Veronica's eye, he quickly moved down the row, feeling slight embarrassment and a few butterflies. He smiled despite himself and turned into the next aisle.

Get it together, he thought. *You got this. Compared to public humiliation and near death, this is cake.* He shook his head to clear his mind, and at that moment walked directly into Veronica, spilling her armful of Marvel movies all over the floor. He apologized profusely, but she simply smiled.

"Hey, Stan-Lee. What's up? Haven't seen you for a few months."

"Yeah," Lloyd said. "I, I haven't been watching many movies lately."

"Oh, yeah?" Veronica said. "Some sort of summer diet of deprivation or something?" she joked.

"Nah. Let's just say," he paused, "I needed to focus a

little more on reality." Lloyd handed her a neat stack of movies and they both stood.

"Aww, that's a shame," she said, her eyes flicking toward him before she turned to begin shelving the movies. "Reality is overrated. But you're looking at movies, so that must mean you're back in the saddle now. Does that mean you're looking for another rom-com to study tonight?"

"Nope. All done with rom-coms, thank you very much. They're on my banned list for the remainder of the year."

"Whew, that's a relief. Kind of boring if you ask me." Veronica continued shelving movies. "Besides, you can find romance in lots of other movies. In fact, you can find romance anywhere," their eyes connected briefly before she turned back to the shelf and gestured. "Case in point: one of my favorites." She pulled a movie off the shelf. "In fact, if you're interested, maybe we can watch it together and discuss the way the romantic dialogue, resonant soundtrack, and special effects intersect. Sometimes what you want is not where you went looking for it." Veronica handed him the movie with a cheeky smile, turned suggestively, and began walking toward the checkout desk.

Lloyd looked down and saw she had handed him *Star Wars: The Empire Strikes Back*. His mouth hung open briefly, then he and his wide smile walked toward the desk with his library card and a pre-written copy of his address and phone number.

~~~
~~~

10,000 Pink Birds of Love Mix Tape

Side 1:

Radiohead – "Morning Bell"

The Verve – "Bittersweet Symphony"

Nelly – "Hot in Herre"

Michael Franti & Spearhead (feat. Cherine Anderson) – "Say Hey (I Love You)"

Al Green – "Let's Stay Together"

Europe – "The Final Countdown"

St Germain – "Rose Rouge"

Side 2:

Van Halen – "Jump"

Marcy Playground – "Sex and Candy"

PINK – "It's All Your Fault"

Julie Delpy – "A Waltz for a Night"

Beck – "Everybody's Got to Learn Sometime"

Bob Dylan or Garth Brooks (but not Billy Joel) – "Make You Feel My Love"

ABOUT THE AUTHOR

Suzan G Brydon is an author, mother, partner, Oxford comma supporter, and Jill of all trades but master of none. Although she has published non-fiction, this book is her first (but certainly not last) attempt at fiction…and for that she apologizes in advance.

She currently resides in Missouri in body and Colorado in spirit and is currently working on the sequel to this book, as well as several forthcoming book projects.

* 9 7 8 0 9 9 7 1 9 8 4 1 6 *